CU00829396

We Don't Care If You're Offended

an anthology

Simon McHardy & Sean Hawker

We Don't Care If You're Offended Copyright © 2023 by **Simon McHardy & Sean Hawker**
All Rights Reserved.

All rights reserved. No part of this book may be reproduced in any form or by any electronic or mechanical means including information storage and retrieval systems, without permission in writing from the author. The only exception is by a reviewer, who may quote short excerpts in a review.

The Day The Music Died. . . And Was Eaten and **WuFlu** first published in **Unamerican Trash: An Unpatriotic Anthology** by godless 2022

Demonectomy first published in **In Uterus: An Anthology for a Friend** by godless 2022

Yoga School Massacre, Munging, Scissors, Blowie, Bunnies, first published
by Potter's Grove Press 2022

Cover design by **Drew Stepek** of godless.com

This book is a work of fiction. Names, characters, places, and incidents either are products of the author's imagination or are used fictitiously. Any resemblance to actual persons, living or dead, events, or locales is entirely coincidental.

First Published March 2023
Potter's Grove Press, LLC

ISBN **978-1-951840-67-9**

CONTENTS

What Have We Got Here

There are some things that one must experience for themselves. Such is this.

Glancing through the table of contents of this anthology, all I can do is shake my head at the wonder of such a collection of depravity gathered in a single volume. Simon McHardy and Sean Hawker typically release these stories in short blasts. A story here, a story there with enough time in between to at least attempt to wash out the stink of vomit and regret from your mouth. Not this time, though. The following compilation fires off one sick yarn after another, a relentless bombardment to the senses and an inevitable destruction of whatever self-defined morality you try so desperately to cling to. The guilt and shame will soak you to your very core as you lose yourself to the humor in things that you never imagined could be funny.

The witty, dark satire aimed at this completely absurd world in which we are living will sting as you are reminded of just how ridiculous, self-absorbed, and soft our society has become. The irony of a self-appointed "moral police" made up entirely of immoral individuals. The self-righteous no longer cackle from the fringes of traditional religion, but from a new religion. The religion of "my truth" reinforced by made-up words and playing make-believe. This collection is precisely what these overly sensitive, *look-at-me-look-at-me* generations need.

Stories such as these are important—they are necessary. They continue to push back on the ever-changing line of what is acceptable. And if there's anything we need in this world, it's that. McHardy and Hawker aren't afraid to thumb their noses at the gatekeepers, to flick a booger at the influencers, and, most importantly, flip a meaty middle finger to everyone and everything. Nothing is safe with these two. Nothing is off-limits. That is what we all need to fight for and continue to preserve and promote. Authors who aren't afraid to offend people. Aren't afraid to piss off the Insta-muh-gram reviewers or the rest of the pearl-clutching masses. Without writers like Hawker and McHardy, we risk slipping into a stale, castrated literary environment that before we know it, we won't be able to write about anything for fear of offending someone, somewhere.

So, if after reading this anthology it turns out that your delicate sensitivities have been offended . . . well, as the title states, We Don't Care. That needs to be the mantra moving forward for all writers desiring to push the envelope of what's acceptable. Forget the social media approval, forget the sensitivity readers. Write what you want. Let Simon and Sean be the example.

We don't care if you're offended. We don't care what you think. You didn't like something you read—good. That's fine. Keep your cry closet stocked with fresh coloring books and move on with your life. It's okay for things to exist that you don't like or agree with. But I'm willing to bet that most of you will enjoy this collection more than you ever imagined you would. You'll gag, you'll laugh, and your jaw will hit the floor more than once but most of all, you'll have fun. And that, my friend, is exactly what we all need to make our time on this spinning dung heap a bit more bearable. Life is difficult enough, why add to it with manufactured offense and faux outrage? Go ahead, feel free to laugh at all the bestiality, dead kids, and trannies you want to but most importantly, remember to laugh at yourself. You're ridiculous, I'm ridiculous, and that's a beautiful thing.

River Dixon
February 16, 2023

The Day The Music Died...
And Was Eaten

(We wanted to put the lyrics to Don McLean's American Pie here but we couldn't because we couldn't get permission from the cunts who own it!)

Anything that walks, swims, crawls, or flies is edible.
Ancient Chinese Proverb

Jape, aka The Big Bopper, staggered down the stairs of the Surf Ballroom and into the crowded dressing room. He collapsed, shivering and pale, into a chair in the far corner. Buddy Holly looked up from polishing his Fender Strat guitar. "You look like shit," he said. Jape sneezed and wiped up the string of thick, green snot with his shirtsleeve. He had the flu, and it had been getting steadily worse. The Midwest was in the grip of a freezing winter. The old bus they'd rented had no heating and was as cold as the interior of an icebox. Carl Bunch, Buddy's drummer, got such bad frostbite that the tour group were forced to leave him behind to recover in a hospital in Ironwood, Michigan.

Buddy was worried about Jape. Another long-distance, frozen bus ride and he'd undoubtedly catch a serious bout of pneumonia. That meant one of the star attractions of The Winter Dance Party tour would be out of commission. The fans would be disappointed. Carl could be replaced, but The Big Bopper certainly couldn't. "I tell you what, Jape, we just charted a private plane to take us to our next gig in Moorhead. Someone might give up his seat to you since you're so sick and all." Buddy raised his eyebrows and looked expectantly at Waylon Jennings, his bassist. Buddy wasn't going to give up his own seat. He'd sell his mother's soul for a chance to do a suitcase full of stinky laundry and get a full night's sleep in a hotel bed.

Big-hearted Waylon looked over at Jape huddled in his chair, sniffling and trembling. "Yeah, okay. The big lout needs it more than me, I guess."

"Thanks, Waylon," Jape spluttered.

Ritchie Valens coughed and raised his puppy-dog eyes at Tommy Allsup, Buddy's guitarist. "How about it, Tommy? You want to give up your seat too? I'm not feeling too hot either." Everyone stared at Tommy who shook his head in disbelief. "I'm really sick," Ritchie said.

"I'll tell you what, I'll toss you for it." Tommy pulled a dime from his pocket and flicked it in the air. "Call it."

"Heads," Ritchie said.

The dime plinked on the floor. "It's heads. Looks like you're coming with us, Ritchie," Buddy remarked, punching the air. Ritchie was as important as The Big Bopper to the tour.

"That's the first time I've ever won anything in my life," Ritchie said, grinning.

"I called a cab to take us to the airport," Buddy said. He shook Waylon's and Tommy's hands. "Well, I hope your ol' bus freezes up again."

"Well, I hope your ol' plane crashes," Waylon replied.

Buddy held out a hand to Jape. The big man wobbled on his feet, and Buddy could barely support him. Ritchie opened the stage door, and a blast of frosty air struck their faces. No screaming fans jostled around the entrance. No admirers had braved the blustery weather for a glimpse of their idols. Buddy was disappointed. Fans would wait hours in a blizzard for Elvis. They bundled Jape into the waiting cab and loaded the suitcases into the trunk. The driver had the heat cranked up, and the boys sighed with pleasure as they breathed in the warm air and began to thaw. Buddy wiped the mist from the window. Surf Ballroom's parking lot was half deserted. "This whole fucking tour is a shit show, man," Buddy whined. "The show wasn't even sold out, and we're the biggest names in rock and roll at the moment." As soon as it was over, he was going to get a new manager, one who knew what the fuck he was doing.

The taxi turned onto a deserted Main Street. By the side of the road, a diner's neon sign lit up the night. Jape pressed his face against the cab window. "Stop the car. I need to get something to eat. I'm starving."

The taxi slowed to a crawl. "Hell no, we're running late. Don't stop, driver," Buddy said. The car sped up again.

"But you know what happens when I get hungry, Buddy."

"Yeah. You become even more of an unbearable asshole than usual," Ritchie said.

"We can't do it, Jape. If we miss this flight, we'll have to take the bus with all the other popsicles. I'm not going to chance getting ill. Plus, there's no refund for the cost of hiring the plane." Buddy was feeling hungry himself. They hadn't eaten since breakfast, but he really didn't want to risk missing the flight. "We'll get something to eat once we land, okay?"

Jape whimpered, "Okay, Buddy."

The snow was falling hard, and a thick mist hung over the Mason City airport. Buddy paid the driver and stepped from the warmth of the cab into an arctic wind blowing across the runway. He hunkered down in his jacket and pulled the collar up over his ears.

"Praise be to Jesus, Mr Holly. It's a pleasure to meet you, sir." A sandy-haired man, around Buddy's age, appeared out of the mist. He gripped Buddy's hand and pumped it furiously. "I'm Roger Peterson. I'll be your pilot." The young man's hand was icy cold. "I'm a huge fan, Mr Holly. It's a real honor to be flying you. If there's anything I can do for you, please let me know."

"Just get us there in one piece," Buddy said, laughing.

"You serving any food on this flight?" Jape asked.

"I'm afraid not. We're not that sort of airline," Roger replied. Jape sniveled, pouted, and looked around the runway as if he expected to see an after-hours diner alongside the flight strip, flashing its 'open' sign through the mist. Buddy and Ritchie gathered up Jape and the baggage and crunched through the slush after Roger. The plane was a six-seater, single engine. The wings were dusted heavily with cement grey snow.

Ritchie peered through the fog. "I thought the plane would be bigger."

"Why? There's only three of us." Buddy's teeth chattered. He was eager to get out of the cold.

"I'm scared of flying. I'm okay on those big jumbo jets, but I've never been on a plane this small."

Buddy raised an eyebrow in concern. The last thing he wanted was Ritchie to get nervous. Everyone knew what Ritchie did when he was stressed. "You'll be alright, Ritchie. We are in the hands of an experienced pilot. Isn't that right, Roger?" He clapped Roger on the shoulder blade as the pilot opened the plane's hatch.

"You betcha, Mr Holly," he replied.

The pilot was a little young, and he had dark circles under his eyes, but Buddy wasn't going to share his misgivings with Ritchie. "Besides, I've got this!" Buddy quipped. He pulled out a hip flask and shook it, sloshing around the liquid inside. "It'll take the edge off and help you to relax."

"I'll have some of that. Gimme." Jape snatched the flask out of Buddy's hand and took a swig. He spat the liquid onto the snow. It looked like piss. "Ugh, what the hell is it?"

"Peach schnapps."

"That's not going to calm a fruit fly." Jape shuddered and hoicked again. They clambered up the air-stairs and followed the pilot into the plane. Buddy tried to elbow his way past Jape, but The Big Bopper pushed him back and sprawled over the two seats behind the cockpit. His head popped up, and he grinned at Buddy who was lowering himself into the vacant seat beside Ritchie. Buddy pulled a face and gave Jape the middle finger. Ritchie stared straight ahead and chewed at the quick of his thumbnail.

The engine coughed into life, and the plane rattled. Ritchie gripped his knees and bit his lip. "It's a short flight, gentlemen, around one hour and fifteen minutes. I'm just waiting on clearance from the tower," Roger yelled.

"It sure beats the bus," Buddy said. "We'll be at the hotel in no time." It was the best one hundred and ten dollars he'd spent on this tour. He could already smell the clean laundry and feel the crisp bed sheets. Sheer bliss.

Jape clutched his stomach. "You sure you don't have something to eat up there? A sandwich? A bag of nuts? A chocolate bar perhaps?"

"No. I've already said I've got nothing," Roger replied.

The radio crackled. "Foxtrot indigo five niner you're clear for take off."

The plane rolled down the runway, picking up speed. Ritchie shifted anxiously in his seat. He wiped a clammy hand across his sweat-beaded brow, and his other hand clutched at the armrest. Buddy offered him the flask. "Schnapps?" Ritchie snatched it and drained the liqueur in two gulps. The plane veered from one side of the narrow runway across to the other as the wheels skidded on the black ice. The plane vibrated, and they were airborne. Wind and snow blasted the cockpit window. The visibility diminished until all they could see was a swirling whiteness.

Jape's stomach growled above the roar of the engine. Ritchie looked out of the window at the veil of white and sucked in rapid breaths. His trembling hands squirmed into his pants. He pulled out his semi-hard cock, spat into his palm, then worked the veiny shaft with long, slow strokes.

Buddy sighed. Every time Ritchie got nervous, he had to rub one out to relax. He did it before every show and sometimes during. Everyone on the tour was used to Ritchie's coping mechanism. One hand strummed his guitar whilst the other beat his meat. Buddy had to admit it was quite an impressive feat, but he would never tell Ritchie that. The rhythm of wet slaps

11

continued to resound in his ears as he closed his eyes and imagined the feel of clean underwear on his skin.

"Hey," Jape said, shaking Buddy's arm and disturbing his reverie. "Do you think the hotel will have room service?"

"I suspect so."

"Man, I hope so, Buddy. I don't know how much longer I can last. I'm sick as a dog, and my guts are eating themselves."

"Don't worry about it, Jape. A couple hours and we'll be dining like kings."

"I just don't want a repeat of what happened in Sheboygan, you know?" Jape whispered.

Buddy pressed his finger to Jape's lips and said, "Shhhh. Forget about Sheboygan. If anyone were to find out about that little incident, we'd be royally fucked. I've got a respectable public image to uphold and a band to keep together. Don't jeopardize that by not keeping your big mouth shut."

Jape nodded and reclined in his seat. Buddy adjusted his eyeglasses. Despite putting up a front, Buddy was worried. They wouldn't arrive at the hotel for at least two hours, and Jape certainly wasn't the kind of guy you wanted to be around when he was hungry. Sheboygan, Wisconsin was a total clusterfuck. They were lucky not to be languishing in a jail cell right now. Buddy loosened his tie. He pressed his thumbs against his temple and rotated them in small circles to ease the tension behind his eyes. His mind cast back to the look of shock on the woman's face, the cries of her baby, and the Pomeranian that just wouldn't stop yapping…

The sound of Ritchie groaning and thwacking his meat grew louder. *He must be on the verge of blowing his load*, Buddy thought. He huddled over in his seat. Ritchie was a heavy cummer, and Buddy didn't want his bandmate splattering him with jizz.

"I just wanted to say how much of a fan I am of your music, Mr Holly. I've followed your career since the beginning," Roger said. "All my friends in our church group think… what the fuck?!" Roger cranked his head around and stared at Ritchie's boner.

"Ritchie always jerks off when he's nervous. It's the only thing that calms him down," Buddy intoned mechanically. He'd given this speech a hundred times in the last week to promoters, club owners, and audiences all over the country. Most folk accepted musicians were a strange bunch.

Roger's eyes bugged out, and his face flushed with rage as he stared at Ritchie's fat, uncut Latino cock. "Masturbation is a sin, and he's going to Hell for such a gratuitous display of self-abuse! Tell him to stop immediately, or I'll turn this thing around."

"You're not one of those bible belt homophobes that gets triggered by the sight of dicks, are you?" Jape asked.

"Ooooh, ooooh, fuck, yeah," Ritchie moaned, working his prick faster and faster until his hand was a blur.

"He's nearly done. Please, just let him finish," Buddy said. "He'll be calm as a millpond afterwards." Jape licked his lips as he fixated on a thick strand of precum that was whipping about wildly from the mouth of Ritchie's cockhead like a rice noodle.

"I said, stop. How dare you offend God with your onanism." Roger clambered over the seat, grabbed Ritchie by the shoulders, and shook him aggressively. "Cease your lascivious exhibition, damn you!"

"Fu-fu-fuck, I'm g-going to c-c-cum… La Bamba!" Ritchie's eyes rolled back in his head. A pearly rope of cock snot shot out and splattered all over Roger's face.

"My eyes," he shrieked. "Jesus Christ, it burns so bad." He rubbed at the willy goo plastering his face and toppled over between the seats whilst the plane pitched and the luggage slewed across the aisle.

"Holy shit, control the fucking plane, Roger," Buddy cried out. He went rigid in his seat as bags and a guitar case rolled past him towards the front of the aircraft.

"Ooh, mamacita," Ritchie moaned, slumping in his seat and stroking his twitching, drooling cock.

"Mmm, it looks and smells like clam chowder," Jape said. He snatched Roger by the head and greedily licked the cum from his face. "It tastes like clam chowder too."

"Arghhh! This is so fucking gay," Roger screamed, flapping his arms about and jumping to his feet.

"The fucking plane, man, the fucking plane," Buddy screamed. The plane's nose dipped until the aircraft was almost vertical. It went into a steep descent and slammed the passengers into the seats in front of them.

"Oh shit." Roger tried to scramble back over the seat into the cockpit, but Jape tugged at him and tongued his face as if it were a melting ice cream.

"Mmm, this is delicious." Roger shoved at Jape to push him away, but The Big Bopper was much too strong. They were going to crash if Buddy didn't do something fast to stop this madman. He flew at Jape and wrestled his arms behind his back until he was forced to release Roger. The pilot dived over the seat and landed head first, his legs thrashing in the air. "I want my clam chowder," Jape yelled, grabbing Roger's legs and trying to yank him upright. "It's so rich and creamy."

"Help me, Ritchie," Buddy cried. "For God's sake, we'll die if we don't stop Jape." His arms were wrapped around Jape's waist, heaving him away from the frantic, cum- and saliva-drenched pilot. All the commotion only added fuel to Ritchie's panic wank. He worked his cock manically whilst he watched the events around him unfold. Through the cockpit window Buddy glimpsed the speck of a farmhouse surrounded by snow-covered fields. The building was fast becoming bigger. Buddy scrambled into his seat and fumbled with the seat belt.

Time stood still the moment the front of the plane slammed into the earth. Buddy, Jape, and Ritchie were tossed around the narrow cabin with the luggage, engulfed in complete darkness. Buddy winced as the banshee screech of metal skidding over solid ground cut through the shuddering gloom. Earth and snow churned at the windows. The aircraft juddered through a field. Buddy's chair was torn from the seat belt rail. He was flung into the air as the fuselage smashed against something solid and was ripped apart near the wing. Buddy was thrown free and cartwheeled through the snow.

Buddy woke, gasping for breath. The icy air felt like glass shards stuffed into his lungs. A winding sheet of snow covered him up to the neck. Gritting his teeth, he managed to move his arms and brush the snow from his frozen body. He struggled to sit up and screamed as a searing pain rippled through his leg. Glancing down, he saw his femur jutting out above his right knee. Red stalactites of frozen blood hung from the protruding bone. "Somebody help me," he croaked. "I'm badly injured." The plane had burrowed along a further two hundred feet from the initial impact point. Its hollow carcass was a smoldering wreck, twisted against a wire fence.

"Oh my god. Ritchie, Jape," Buddy moaned. He tried to haul himself up but collapsed back into the thick carpet of snow. On the second attempt, he managed to stand, and dragging his mangled leg, he shuffled along the furrows of dirt where the plane had harvested a crop of late turnips. He followed their strips of white flesh to the smoking ball of crumpled steel. Buddy shook his head at the sad irony. Turnips were the only food Jape absolutely refused to eat. Clouds of tar-black smoke drifted slowly into the grey sky, and the acrid taste of hot oil scorched his tongue. His leg was freezing, numbing the worst of the pain. It looked fucked though. He needed emergency treatment fast.

When he drew near the wreckage, he sighted a large figure with a distended belly hunched over a mound on the snow. "Jape, is that you?" Buddy croaked. His voice was a hoarse whisper, and he had to shout again above the howling wind.

The Big Bopper spun around with strings of bloody meat dangling from his mouth. Strips of singed, tattered cloth were draped over his shoulders; the flames had reduced most of his clothes to ash. His skin, red and scalded, glistened with a sickening sheen of second and third degree burns. The top of his head, scorched bald, emitted a nimbus of smoke. Buddy gazed at the heap of gore-covered bones littered at Jape's unshod feet. Jape squatted over the pile and picked up the remnants of a severed arm. The hand still clutched a crispy, black penis, a barbecued sausage on the end of a stick. "Poor Ritchie," Buddy muttered solemnly. Jape bit into the charred cock, chewed hungrily, and swallowed.

"Need more meat," moaned Jape, standing up and lumbering towards Buddy. This was the worst he'd ever seen Jape. Even in Sheboygan, he'd eaten the woman, her baby, and the dog with a certain finesse. Now he'd descended to the behavioral level of a savage jungle beast. Buddy scanned the site for any sign of the pilot before he retreated through the snow. His shoes sank into the ground. He could drag himself across the field only a few inches at a time and picked up a small V-shaped branch to use as a crutch.

Jape staggered after him with his arms outstretched like a zombie. "Need more meat," he repeated. "So hungry, Buddy." Adrenaline surged through Buddy, and he jammed his crutch into the ground and limped to the distant farmhouse, his leg hanging off at the knee joint. He glanced over his shoulder and saw The Big Bopper close on his tail. "Hold up, Buddy. I just want to talk."

"No, you don't. You want to eat me."

Painful, throbbing heat flooded through his broken leg. Jape was so close Buddy could hear his teeth graunching on bone splinters and smell his meaty jowls. The ruined leg became a deadweight, and Buddy was forced to hop with his crutch. Jape's huge arm lashed out and grabbed at Buddy's torn clothes. He ripped the jacket and shirt off Buddy's torso, forcing him to turn around and face him. "What the fuck is that?" Jape said.

Protruding from the center of Buddy's chest was a head the size of a large apple. A flabby, pale arm poked out underneath Buddy's left nipple. The face looked like a plastic mask that had been bleached in the sun, but it resembled Buddy and even had thick, horn-rimmed glasses and a teddy boy haircut. The head grinned sheepishly at The Big Bopper. "I'm Chester, Buddy's twin. I do all the singing because Buddy's voice is garbage."

Jape furrowed his brow, at a loss for words.

"It's true," Buddy said. He sang a line from *Peggy Sue*.

Chester was right. Buddy's voice sounded like a goat being sodomized by a wine bottle.

"But how do you it? You know, on stage without anyone noticing?" Jape got closer and prodded Chester to see if he was real.

"Buddy gives me a mic. He hides it under his shirt. I hold it in my little hand, see." Chester opened and closed his tiny fist. "He makes sure his mic is disconnected and then I do all the singing. Buddy just mouths the words."

Jape scratched his head. Burnt flesh peeled away under his finger nails. "Does Arlene know about this, Buddy?"

"Of course she does," Buddy replied.

"The three of us get on really well actually, especially in the bedroom, a-hey, hey." Chester made a rude gesture with two of his fingers and Buddy blushed.

"Wow. Well, that's all very interesting, pal, but I need more meat." He lunged at Buddy and seized Chester's arm. Chester screamed, and Buddy jerked away, dropping his crutch and hollering.

Jape pulled Buddy and Chester into the snow and tore into his abdomen, snarling and salivating. "Don't do this, Jape. I can't live without Buddy. I'm a parasitic twin. The music will die."

The vacant-eyed Big Bopper ignored Chester's pleas and thrust his face into the cavity. He latched onto an intestine, bit into the juicy tube, and slurped. His huge fist burrowed under the fleshy, purple rope, and he scooped out yard after yard of entrails and crammed them into his mouth.

"The world needs us," Buddy spluttered, folding his arms protectively over his chest.

Batting away Buddy's hands, Jape yanked Chester's arm off and ripped the meat from the little limb with his canines. He chomped down on Chester's head, spitting out clumps of hair soaked in bay-rum scented pomade as well as the miniature pair of eyeglasses. Jape tore into Buddy's ribs, turning him over like a corncob. He cracked the chest cavity open, wrenched out the lungs and Buddy's pulsing heart, and bit into it. The leaking tubes flapped and oozed blood over his quivering chin.

Buddy saw a line of troopers on the horizon, approaching them with guns drawn. It was too late for him, but Chester might be okay. He was a tough ol' boy. If he could be saved, maybe the music wouldn't have to die after all. The silhouette of a trooper levelled his rifle and fired. A single shot rang out into the vast expanse of open sky, startling the birds high up in the trees. The Big Bopper sneezed then his head exploded into several large pieces of brain and skull, painting the snow next to Buddy a bright shade of scarlet.

YOGA SCHOOL MASSACRE

Harriet hated going to the doctor. The waiting room was packed full of ailing and decrepit bodies. Overhead, the ceiling fan did little to alleviate the almost intolerable humidity, but it did successfully circulate the old people smell. The hum of its whirling blades was muted by the cacophony of bronchial coughs and the incessant ringing of the telephones. Her armpits and inner thighs were clammy and chafed from repeated rubbing. She needed to get the weight off her feet. Her shoulders slumped and she groaned as she scanned the room for an unoccupied seat or two.

The receptionist looked up and gave Harriet a dead-eyed smile. She bustled from behind her desk and whispered to two old-aged pensioners seated on the double bench closest to the corridor that led off to the doctors' offices. Harriet heard the man complain loudly about the unfairness of very fat people being given priority seating over the elderly. The receptionist nodded, and after a few more gripes, they reluctantly vacated their seats and hobbled away. Harriet squeezed past and sank onto the warm bench. The usual snide remarks and stares followed her. She knew what they were all thinking: You wouldn't be here if you didn't stuff your fat face with burgers, pizzas, and kebab meat all the time.

They were right too. She pretended she was happy, but her body was rebelling against her strict diet of hourly takeaways and greasy snacks. At three hundred and eighty pounds, she looked like the Michelin Man after he'd been locked in a pie shop for a week. During Harriet's last visit for a nasty yeast infection,

Doctor Fothergill-Brown cautioned her that if she didn't lose weight, she wouldn't make thirty. The women's group she belonged to had scoffed at the doctor's warning and assured her that being a person of a larger body did not lead to health problems. Recently she'd been plagued with thundering migraines and lower back pain. When her aching leg joints could barely carry her to the fridge, Harriet began to question her undying loyalty to the group and booked another appointment for a check-up.

"Miss Harriet Hambeast?" the receptionist called over the din. It was an unfortunate surname, and several people in the waiting room sniggered.

"Yes," she said, her cheeks flushing pink. She lowered her head, compressing her many chins, and stared at her blotchy, ulcerated feet and the blubbery, purple fat spilling out of the open-toed sandals.

"The doctor's ready to see you now. Room four, please," the receptionist said. Harriet struggled to her feet with a grunt. The bench rose with her, wedged to her ass. "Leave the bench, please, Miss Hambeast. The doctor has a very large chair ready for you in his office." The sniggering morphed into uproarious laughter.

Harriet yanked herself out of the seat and let it clunk to the ground. She waddled from the waiting room, feeling every set of eyes boring into her. Dr Fothergill-Brown's office was at the end of the long corridor. She shuffled along as hastily as she could, and by the time she tapped on the half-opened door, her vast bosom was heaving in protest, and her forehead was dotted with beads of sweat. "Come in," a lugubrious voice instructed. She entered the room nervously. Dr Fothergill-Brown's tall, bony frame was folded into his chair. A few strands of grey hair clung to the sallow skin stretched over his large, angular skull. "Ah, Miss Hambeast," he said, flicking his eyes over her. "Shut the door, please. It's good to see you are still among the living. If you'd be so kind as to undress and get on the scales." He waved his spindly hand in the air where it fluttered like a bird.

Harriet stripped down to her parachute-sized panties and bra and climbed up onto the scales. The numbers clicked over and over. Doctor Fothergill-Brown sidled up beside her. "Four hundred and five pounds, Miss Hambeast. You've put on weight. A lot of weight."

"That's not what's causing my headaches and sore knees, doctor. My weight gain could be due to any number of reasons. I may have fluid retention. My thyroid might be malfunctioning, or my bones may have thickened and got bigger."

"If by fluid retention you mean an Oreo cheesecake milkshake lining up behind a pint of caramel custard, then I'm sure you're correct, Miss Hambeast. If by bigger bones you mean swapping deep-fried chicken wings for giant turkey drumsticks with an extra-large bucket of fries on the side, then I may be inclined to agree." All this talk of food made Harriet's stomach rumble. "As for your thyroid, we checked that last time you were here." Doctor Fothergill-Brown returned to his desk and tapped away on his keyboard, shaking his head despondently. "Get dressed and have a seat next to me, Miss Hambeast," he huffed.

Harriet clambered off the scales. She struggled into her elasticised trousers and voluminous smock top, then sat on the chair next to Doctor Fothergill-Brown. Harriet gripped the armrests in fear the chair might collapse from under her. The doctor swivelled around and peered at her over the top of his wire-framed spectacles, "Let's check your blood pressure now." He selected the extra-large adult cuff size and fitted it around her fleshy arm.

Harriet gritted her teeth as the cuff throttled her upper arm. "Two hundred and five over one ten. That's the cause of your headaches," Doctor Fothergill-Brown said.

"What about my aching joints?"

"Your joints are aching and swollen because they are supporting over four hundred pounds of weight. You're a beast... sorry, I mean obese. Morbidly so. I advised you last time that if you didn't lose a significant amount of weight, you'd be at an increased risk of having a massive heart attack or stroke. Type 2 Diabetes is inevitable at this stage as well."

"But HEFFER said that's completely wrong. Fat has no direct correlation with any of those health issues."

"HEFFER, Miss Hambeast?" Doctor Fothergill-Brown leaned closer to Harriet and steepled his bony fingers against his top lip.

"Yes, HEFFER is an online women's group I belong to that promotes body positivity. The name stands for Helping Every Fatty Fight for Equal Rights. They said we need to reclaim what were once pejoratives like 'Fatty' and 'Blubber Butt' and embrace them in a positive way to combat the social stigma of being a person of a larger body."

"You mean 'obese', Miss Hambeast."

Harriet wagged her finger at him. "No, no, no. We don't use that word. It's akin to using the N-word in front of a person of colour."

Doctor Fothergill-Brown removed his glasses and rubbed his eyes. "A rose by any other name would smell just as sweet, Miss Hambeast, and what we are talking about is a rose that weighs the equivalent of a pygmy hippo." Harriet squirmed. "Obesity has everything to do with your health. These people are deluded. They don't care about you. They have no self-discipline and will use any excuse to indulge themselves and take others down with them."

"What you're saying is not fair, doctor. It's discrimination. Fat shaming."

Doctor Fothergill-Brown sighed. "No, it's reality. Being fat is not healthy and lowers your life expectancy by up to twenty years. A plethora of scientific evidence supports this." The doctor swung back to his computer.

Harriet's bottom lip and triple chins quivered. Come to think of it the profile photos of other members of HEFFER showed them as not looking particularly healthy or happy. She always had an inkling that the whole block of cheese they recommended she melt on her breakfast bowl of French fries wasn't good for her. "What should I do, doctor?"

The doctor printed out a script and then reached into his drawer. He selected a pamphlet and handed it to Harriet with the prescription for her high blood pressure medication. "Here are some suggestions for healthy, low-calorie meals. Have you been exercising at all? Walking? Going to the gym?" She could see in his eyes that he realised this was a stupid question the moment it escaped his lips.

"I don't like walking. It hurts my knees. I used to go to the gym, but there was a problem with my membership, and they had to cancel it indefinitely." Harriet didn't mention how she hated the way people stopped and stared as she jiggled along the street. Nor did she mention she'd been banned from the gym after she was caught stealing bodybuilders' protein shakes to pour over her chocolate puddings in between reps on the weight machines.

"Have you ever considered yoga?"

"Isn't that some sort of low-fat dessert, doctor?"

"No, Miss Hambeast. It's a gentle form of exercise. It would help with your social anxiety too. The classes are small and some are even women only."

That didn't sound too bad at all. There'd be no men around snickering at her in a leotard. "Do you know of one nearby?" Harriet felt awkward on the bus surrounded by people and had trouble fitting into a car. She mostly stayed home, spending her disability pension on confectionery websites.

"There's a new school just opened up approximately five minutes' walk from here. In your case, allow fifteen minutes. You may have seen the billboard outside. It's a wellness centre called Om-Believable."

"Oh yes, it's near my house." She leaned forward in her chair. "Do you really think it will help, doctor?"

"I've heard excellent reports from several patients," Doctor Fothergill-Brown said, his eyes still glued to the computer screen. "I'm sure their programs will be of assistance to you. It's imperative you do everything in your power to lose weight, Miss Hambeast. Your life depends on it."

Harriet was so inspired she decided to pop into the wellness centre on the way home. To keep her strength up, she made a spontaneous decision to visit the Chin Soon Fatt Chinese Restaurant for the all-you-can-eat buffet beforehand. The owner, Suk Fatt Kok, was outside, opening the restaurant for lunch. He looked up, saw Harriet heading in his direction, and blocked the doorway. "You go way, lady. You eat too much."

Harriet tried to shoulder him out of the way. "You can't stop me, Mr Fatt Kok. It's discrimination." Suk Fatt Kok didn't budge. The delicious aroma of exotic spices wafted through the open door and teased Harriet's tastebuds. "Please, Mr Fatt Kok, I'm starving. I had to go to the doctor this morning, so I missed breakfast. He's very concerned about my health. He said I'm very ill." She batted her eyelashes at him. "I'm only having a snack today. I'm on a diet."

"You say last time. Then food all gone." Harriet drooled. Over Suk Fatt Kok's shoulder, she could see mounds of glistening sweet and sour pork, succulent slices of Peking duck, chicken chow mein, egg tarts, and shrimp dumplings awaiting her. She tried her best to look weak and dizzy from hunger. Suk Fatt Kok's furrowed brow relaxed slightly. "You only use saucer, lady. One, two plates, no more. One saucer only."

Harriet nodded and hurried into the restaurant, bulldozing Suk Fatt Kok to the ground. He struggled to his feet, dusted himself off, and tottered after her, wailing and wringing his hands. As soon as Harriet got to the feed troughs, Suk Fatt Kok tried to push a child's plate into her hand. Harriet ignored him and grabbed the largest plate available. "Please, lady, you ruin me." She piled her plate as high as she could, scooped up the entire tray of shrimp dumplings, then made a beeline for the table closest to the buffet so she'd have less distance to travel for seconds, thirds, and even fourths. She hoovered up the food while Suk Fatt Kok fluttered around her, squeaking his protests in Mandarin.

The two waiters leaning against the bar watched Harriet stuff her gob with all manner of victuals whilst she barely paused for breath. "Tā chī dé tài duō le!" one waiter gasped.

"Tā chī de bǐ xióngmāo hái duō," replied the other waiter, mouth agape.

After Harriet licked her plate clean, she fished around in her purse for the money and dropped the coins onto the dish coated thickly in her saliva. She lurched across the restaurant, sucking on the remains of a barbecued spare rib. "You banned, lady. Too greedy, too greedy!" Suk Fatt Kok yelled after her as she wobbled out of the door. Harriet gave a contented sigh and followed it with a hearty belch. Now she had made up for missing her breakfast, she was ready to enquire about yoga.

Om-Believable peeped from behind a jungle-like garden. Bees hummed, and the heavy scent of blossoms pervaded the air. A bougainvillea with vibrant purple flowers sprawled over a low picket fence and partially smothered a carpet of camomile flowers. Giant cabbage tree palms rustled in the afternoon breeze. Harriet trod down the garden path flanked by moss-covered statues of Hindu deities. A large pond brimming with strange, sharp-teethed fish sparkled in the centre of the lawn. She peered into the water. "Are those piranhas?" she asked herself.

As she drew closer, the wellness centre revealed itself. A huge veranda stretched across the front of a Victorian villa painted daffodil yellow. Rainbows of light from hanging crystals danced around her and wind chimes tinkled above. Harriet closed her eyes and breathed deeply. It was peaceful here. She heaved herself up the porch stairs and paused for breath before reaching for the brass knocker in the shape of an elephant.

The door swung open, and Harriet gazed into a pair of deep blue eyes. Full, pink lips buried in the centre of a luscious, bushy beard curved into a reassuring smile. She blinked, and her eyes swept up to a halo of frizzy golden hair. "Namaste," the man said, palming his hands together and bowing his head. A silky white shirt billowed open to his waist and revealed a golden medallion glinting among a tangle of greying chest hair. Bright orange parachute pants completed the ensemble.

"Hi," Harriet replied, bowing in imitation. The weight of her stomach made her stumble forward, and she had to use the door to steady herself. "I-I'm Harriet. I'm here for yoga."

"Welcome, Harriet. I am Sandyrama Sai Baba. It is a pleasure to make your acquaintance this fine day. Please come inside." He stepped to the edge of the doorway. Harriet could barely squeeze through, but Sandyrama's smile never wavered as he watched her struggle past him. A cloud of patchouli and manly musk engulfed her as Sandyrama laid his hand on her shoulder and guided her along a hallway, plush with thick Persian carpets, into a sunlit room. Leadlight windows projected mellow greens and blues across a polished kauri floor. Half a dozen hemp yoga mats were arranged around the room.

Large cages housing exotic animals lined the walls. "Oh my god." Harriet's jaw dropped and she stopped abruptly.

"Magnificent, aren't they? We harness their primal energy when we practise yoga." Sandyrama's hand increased the pressure on her shoulder as he pushed her gently to a cage where a baboon slept with its huge, bright red ass squashed against the steel mesh. The animal woke up with a start, turned, and bared its dagger-like fangs. Harriet gasped and stumbled against Sandyrama. "You're trembling like a leaf." His body leaned into hers, and his arm dropped from her shoulder to encircle her waist. He fondled a handful of the fat roll hanging over her waistband.

"Sorry, your pet monkey startled me."

"These creatures aren't pets. I keep them wild to maintain their raw power," he breathed. "Once we are in the full, uninterrupted flow of our yoga, we can feel their spiritual energy blend in harmony with our own and open up the seven chakras of the body. Amazing, right?"

"Oh yes, very." Harriet had no idea what he was talking about.

"Come and meet the others. Do you like large serpents?" Harriet felt a hard bulge press against the small of her back. "This is a black mamba, the most venomous snake in the world. One drop of its venom can kill ten men." Harriet peered into the glass tank at the jet-black serpent coiled up under a heat bulb.

"He's cute."

Sandyrama laughed a deep throaty laugh. "And his neighbour is a Burmese python capable of squeezing over six pounds of pressure per square inch. This one's powerful enough to crush the ribs of a bull." Sandyrama squeezed Harriet's waist tightly, making her giggle. "I have to keep an eye on him; he can get a bit frisky." He ushered her over to the next cage. "Here is my pièce de résistance, a Komodo dragon." Harriet gazed in awe at the giant lizard sprawled in its lair that ran the length of the wall. "A million-year-old apex predator. It paralyses its prey with toxic saliva and then eats it alive. The energy one acquires from this magnificent creature is astounding."

"What's that?" Harriet pointed to a horn poking out of a glutinous ball in the middle of the cage.

"The remains of a goat. The Komodo regurgitates any horns, hooves, hair, and teeth in a mucus ball after it has finished digesting its meal. We have to feed him only once a month. He eats eighty percent of his body weight in one sitting."

What an amateur, Harriet thought. She was sure she'd just eaten her entire body weight, if not more, at the Chinese restaurant.

Sandyrama spun Harriet around and held her at arms' length, his eyes lingering on her gigantic bosom. "Why do you want to learn yoga, Harriet?"

"My doctor says I could do with losing a little weight and that yoga will help me." Harriet fluttered her eyelashes. Sandyrama licked his lips. She went weak at her already weak knees. A man hadn't paid her this much attention since the Nigerian prince who mysteriously disappeared after she sent him a thousand dollars for his airfare to Australia so they could be married.

"Yes. You are fat. In body but not in mind. Yoga will help you with your physical issues and soothe your soul. You must start as soon as possible." Harriet was surprised by his honesty. There was something about Sandyrama's confident charm that said if anyone was going to help her lose weight, he would. "Ladies' classes start at six o'clock every morning, but you will need more than just yoga to help you." He opened a cupboard and selected several jars from the shelves lined with containers of dried plants. "This is traditional Ayurvedic medicine, and it will greatly facilitate your weight loss."

Harriet mouthed the strange words on the labels: Guggulu, Swarn Makshik Bhasm, Shilajit. "Is it safe because I don't do drugs?"

"Ayurvedic medicine has been around for centuries." Sandyrama shook a small portion from each container into a paper bag and handed her the mixture. "It is a very potent medicine. You need to add only a pinch to a cup of boiling water, let it steep for a few minutes, and sip the beverage with your breakfast."

"Thank you so much." She clasped the magic brew to her bosom. "What do I owe you?"

Sandyrama smiled and held Harriet in as tight an embrace as her wide frame would allow. "Nothing, but you owe Goddess Durga, the universal mother, the embodiment of pure force, your commitment and diligence to the sacred art of yoga. So come tomorrow dressed in yoga pants. All girls must wear tight yoga pants to do yoga properly."

Harriet woke at five the next morning. Her mouth was dry and dusty. She reached for the open bottle of Coco-Cola on the bedside table, took a swig, and gargled the soft drink as if it were mouthwash. After brushing the stale crusts left over from a late-night jumbo pizza off the sheets, she heaved herself up in the bed, grunting from the strain. Hidden in the crevices of her fat, Harriet discovered a moist slice of pepperoni and jammed it into her mouth.

Target didn't have any crop tops for larger women, but she'd treated herself to a plus-size tunic top. The blue matched the colour of Sandyrama's eyes, and the shade looked good against her dark brown hair. The yoga pants she'd found in the special out-sized range fitted snugly, but there was still some room for the breakfast chocolate cake in the fridge. "Oops, I better have my medicine first." A smile swept over her lips, and she felt a stirring in her loins as she remembered the way Sandyrama pressed his hard body against hers. She shook a generous amount of the magic brew into a teapot and poured in the boiling water. "Now I'll be able to eat all of the cake without getting any fatter," she said as she retrieved the fudgy concoction from the fridge. Once the mixture was cool enough, she strained the mud-like elixir into a mug and tried to gulp it down. The sludge slithered down her throat. Moments later, a bitter aftertaste bubbled angrily up her gullet.

Harriet gagged, grabbed the cake with two hands, and mashed it into her mouth. The rich, chocolatey goodness subdued the taste of her rancid medicine, but just to make sure, she chomped on an entire pack of chocolate biscuits as well.

Harriet's new outfit was drenched with perspiration by the time she arrived at the yoga school. Several expensive sportscars were parked outside along the street. The sun had not yet risen, and fairy lights glowed along the cobble pathway winding through the wild garden. Her stomach fizzled and spasmed. She swallowed down the bile searing her throat. Something nasty was brewing in her stomach. She clenched her sphincter and attempted to release a quiet, controlled fart before entering the building. A long, violent ripple escaped from her anus. It was as if her asshole were screaming. The noise bounced off the trees, but fortunately, no one was waiting around outside Om-Believable to hear it.

Harriet checked her wristwatch. The class was about to begin. Another fart was desperate to escape, but she would have to hold it in for the next forty-five minutes. The door was open and she stepped inside. An overpowering aroma of freshly lit incense drifted through the hallway. She could hear the baboon chattering over the hum of conversation in the main room. Half a dozen slender women, clad in designer yoga pants and crop tops, limbered up next to their mats. Sandyrama, dressed in rich silks, twirled among them, adjusting poses and murmuring encouragement to each lady in turn. He looked up as Harriet shuffled in through the entranceway. "Ah, it's good you returned. I like a big challenge." The women grimaced and exchanged glances. Harriet waved but no one waved in return.

"Take your places on the yoga mats, ladies. Let's begin this morning's session." Harriet waddled over to an unoccupied yoga mat and stood nervously between two women at the rear of the class. Sandyrama dropped down effortlessly into the lotus position at the front of the room. The beautiful women gracefully copied him. Harriet flopped onto the mat like a horse that had been shot and barely managed to cross her tree-trunk legs.

"Close your eyes, ladies, breathe deeply and surrender yourself to the higher power. Om," Sandyrama intoned. The women joined in the chant. Harriet's distressed gut gurgled. She opened one eye and peered around the room, wondering where the toilet was.

"Now move into butterfly stretch to open up those hips, ladies." Sandyrama scanned the multitude of female groins facing him. "Good, open those legs as wide as you can." Harriet drew her heels towards her crotch and tried to push her thighs to the floor like the other girls, but her knees stubbornly pointed to the ceiling however hard she tried. Her cunt slit sucked up the fabric of her yoga pants and gave her a noticeable camel toe.

A fart squeaked out from between the yoga mat and her buttocks. The putrid odour stank like a food waste bin full of spoiled veg. The women on either side of her twitched their nostrils and glared. Harriet averted her eyes. Sandyrama sprang up and glided around the class, helpfully adjusting the spread of women's legs by pressing down on their thighs, his face inches away from their breasts.

"Okay, ladies, bottoms up. Let's move into downward dog." The women all assumed a pose with their heads down and their pert derrières in the air. Harriet was unsure about how this position would affect her bowels, but she could see Sandyrama looking at her expectantly. She rolled onto her sore, creaky knees, grunted, and pushed her bottom up. Blood surged to her head, and waves of dizziness and nausea washed over her. Her huge, drooping belly almost touched the mat, and it let out a long, rumbling growl that echoed through the room.

The excited baboon shook the cage and bared its fangs. "Ah, the baboon's energy is starting to entwine with our own. Very good," Sandyrama announced. "Channel the monkey, ladies, channel the monkey."

Harriet's large colon felt as if it were having a seizure. She urgently needed to use the toilet, or she was going to have an accident all over her yoga mat. "Excuse me, Mr Rama." She put one hand up, lost her balance, and nearly toppled over.

"You need to centre your energy, Harriet," Sandyrama said, sidling up to her. He slipped his hand under her top and pressed firmly on her squishy belly.

"I need to go to the…"

"Just relax. Slowly breathe in and out." He pushed harder on her stomach.

"Please, I…"

"Breathe, Harriet, breathe. Channel the monkey."

"I really must go…"

"The monkey, Harriet. The monkey. Be one with it." Sandyrama peered over the horizon of Harriet's back. "Okay, ladies, shift into ocelot pose. Legs in the air, hands underneath your bums. Spread those cheeks."

Harriet bit her lip as a tidal wave of hot, liquid shit whooshed through her colon and jammed against her sphincter. She clenched her buttocks so tightly she could crack a coconut. "Please, Mr Rama, I need to go now."

Sandyrama grasped Harriet's hips and ground his crotch against her ass cheeks. The nub of his cock wedged between her crack as he pulled her toward him. "Relax, Harriet, you're too tense. Your energy needs to be unblocked. This is a method taught to me during my pilgrimage to the Ganges by a hundred-year-old yogi who lived in a cave." Sandyrama started to dry hump Harriet, thrusting his hips, pounding her wobbly ass.

Harriet's anus exploded. A volcanic eruption of shit and gas spewed from a split in her yoga pants. Sandyrama jerked in fright, his belly and silk trousers slimed in molten faecal matter. Green-black in colour, the liquid stool was an amalgamation of exotic, medicinal herbs, and a whole chocolate cake. Everyone in the class turned and stared silently at her.

"Oh no," Harriet screamed, clasping her shit-drenched ass and struggling to stand up.

"She's shat herself," a skinny woman with no tits and a pallid complexion yelled.

"Fuck, I'm covered in shit," Sandyrama bellowed, the steam rising from his soiled outfit.

Harriet sloshed across the room with liquid faeces squirting from between her fingers. The torrent leaked from the legs of her tight pants then bubbled over the waistband and splashed to the floor. The women huddled together in a group, holding their yoga mats as shields. Everyone retched and spluttered at the thick smog of fetid faecal stink permeating the air. The baboon jumped about wildly and flung pieces of its own shit around its steel cage. "I'm so sorry, Mr Rama. I need to use the bathroom."

"Just fucking leave. Now!" Sandyrama ran down the hallway in front of Harriet and barred her way to the ladies' toilet.

Harriet squelched to the front door and left behind a trail of diarrhoea on the Persian carpet. What was she thinking choosing white yoga pants? The slow, uncomfortable walk home was humiliating. Cars beeped their horns, and passers-by yelled obscenities and laughed. She dropped her head down in shame and sobbed. Harriet would never be able to live this down. She'd be forced to move to another town far away. As soon as she got home, she stripped naked in the yard and flung her mucky clothes into the rubbish bin. She used the garden hose to rid herself of the worst of the sundried shit that'd turned to the consistency of clay.

The next-door neighbour's kids pointed and laughed from the sanctuary of a treehouse. Nude, Harriet shuffled inside to use the shower. Diarrhoea continued to dribble from her asshole until late in the afternoon. By teatime, Harriet's stomach had recovered, but for the first time in her life, she didn't feel like eating. She sat in a lounge chair by the window. A girl in black activewear jogged past with her sleek, high ponytail bobbing up and down. Harriet gazed at her long, muscular legs and taut tummy visible below her crop top. She'd dreamt this would be her after she joined the yoga school, but now her hopes were forever dashed.

An old man shuffled by with his fat, wheezing dog. The dog sniffed at the lamp post and managed to raise his hind leg a few inches before he gave up and squatted down to piss. Harriet had felt just like the poor mutt during the yoga class. "Maybe 'Home and Away' will cheer me up," she sighed. She turned from the window and jabbed at the remote control. Harriet's eyes widened in horror as she noticed a familiar sight on the television screen.

"I'm Justine Henley reporting live from the Om-Believable Yoga School where there's been a report of a chemical weapons attack." A police helicopter hovered overhead, and a crew in biohazard outfits approached the entrance to the wellness centre. The pretty, blond reporter continued to speak directly at the camera. "A yoga school is where you'd expect to find peace and harmony, but not today. Today the school is the scene of domestic terrorism. I'm here with the owner, Sandyrama Sai Baba."

Sandyrama waltzed into the frame. "Namaste, Justine." He'd changed into a lavender open-necked shirt. A pair of black tights showcased his moose knuckle.

"Namaste, Sandyrama Sai Baba. Now, I understand your business has been the target of an abhorrent biological attack. Can you tell us what happened?"

"It was horrible, Justine. A sickeningly obese terrorist burst into our morning class whilst we were meditating, shouted 'Fat is beautiful!' and shat over everyone."

"That's awful. I can't believe such a shambolic excuse for a human being would do such a disgusting thing. You poor man."

"She even shat on my exotic pets. The odour was the foulest I'd ever smelled. I'm going to have to close the school so the industrial cleaners can sort out the mess. She ruined my kauri floor." Sandyrama fingered the gold chain around his neck and ogled Justine's breasts.

"Tragic." Justine shook her blond curls. "Why would they target your business?"

"It was an obvious terror attack on my people."

"Your people?" Justine's eyes sprang wide open, and she pressed the microphone closer to Sandyrama.

"Fit people with a healthy body fat percentage."

"Was anyone injured?" Justine asked.

"I believe all my clients who witnessed the attack will have sustained serious, long-lasting mental and spiritual injuries. The damage to their psyches is unfathomable."

"I'm not a terrorist. It was your magic brew, fucker," Harriet screamed and hurled her slipper at the television. It missed and hit the urn containing her mother's ashes on the mantlepiece.

"Will you reopen your business, and are you afraid of more unprovoked violence by fat people?"

"Shiva willing, Justine, Shiva willing. Yes, I am frightened but courage only exists in the face of adversity. I will not cower in fear and be silenced by the angry fatties of the world." Justine stroked Sandyrama's arm tenderly. "Expect it to be business as usual come Monday morning."

"Lying bastard." Harriet threw her other slipper at the television. It bounced off the screen and went sailing through the open window. She wasn't part of any fatty terrorist organisation. She was the real victim here. She was the one being bullied. All her life she'd been ridiculed because of her weight. HEFFER had made her feel good about herself and given her a sense of belonging. Then the doctor had forced her off to yoga school, and Sandyrama had poisoned her and tried to turn her into a contortionist.

Harriet turned off the television and flung the remote onto the coffee table. She stomped to the kitchen and yanked open the fridge door. Her plump fingers grabbed an enormous leg of pork, and she ripped the juicy meat from the bone with her canine teeth. A loud knocking at the door disturbed Harriet's mastication. She waddled over and released the latch. Two uniformed officers stood on the threshold. "Yeah?" Harriet mumbled, spitting morsels of pig meat at the police.

"Miss Harriet Hambeast?" the female officer asked. Her eyes immediately locked onto the pork leg Harriet clutched in her hand.

"Yeah, who wants to know?" Harriet tore off another hunk of meat.

"I'm Officer Jenkins, and this is Officer Morris." She waved her hand in the direction of her smirking colleague. "We'd like you to accompany us to the police station to answer a few questions."

"What about?" No way this was about the incident at the yoga school. All she was guilty of was accidentally shitting herself in public.

"We have reason to believe you were involved in an, ahem, incident at the Om-Believable Yoga School this morning."

"What? No. Mr Rama gave me this herbal concoction to drink, and it made me have the shits really bad. You can't arrest someone for having explosive diarrhoea." Harriet retreated from the threshold and attempted to shut the door, but Officer Morris planted his large boot in the doorway.

"We take these sorts of attacks on our country very seriously, Miss Hambeast. The biohazard emergency response team had to be called into the yoga school, and the street was closed off to traffic in both directions. Many people involved in the incident are suffering from severe trauma and require medical attention. If you are unwilling to accompany us to the police station, we will have to arrest you on the charge of being a suspected terrorist," Officer Jenkins said coldly.

Harriet reluctantly walked with the officers to the riot van parked outside her house. A crowd had gathered around the vehicle. Harriet noticed people peering from behind their curtains at her. Her face flushed with embarrassment. "Has she been stealing food again?" a man asked.

"Keep away, thank you, sir," Officer Morris replied.

"I bet she didn't pay for that pork leg."

Harriet turned an even brighter shade of scarlet when she looked down and saw she still gripped onto the half-consumed cut of cooked meat. She handed it over to Officer Jenkins and hung her head. Harriet hesitated when Officer Morris slid open the van door. The acrid reek of piss wafted out. She'd never been arrested before. Her heart thumped against her ribs, and her stomach jittered. "I can assure you, you'll be quite comfortable, Miss Hambeast. When dispatch notified us that we were collecting an obese person of interest, we brought the riot van especially. It seats up to six people. Unfortunately, it was used earlier this morning to round up a bunch of drunken football hooligans who couldn't hold their bladders on their way to the cells. Apologies about the smell. Here, let me help you. You look as though you need to sit down. There's a dry spot over there."

Surprisingly, the next morning Harriet was allowed to go home on bail. She'd never been so humiliated in all her life. The police had placed her in a crowded jail cell initially, but when the rumour got around that she was the 'Toxic Spiller', the other inmates kicked up a fuss and threatened to riot unless the officers relocated her.

She had to be transferred to solitary confinement for the other prisoners' protection. They were scared to share a cell with a suspected terrorist whose asshole was classified as a potentially deadly weapon. A court appearance for first thing Monday morning was quickly scheduled, and the lawyer said Harriet should expect to face a significant amount of jail time. He asked her if she owned or rented her house because she would probably also be slapped with some hefty fines.

Her bowel explosion at Om-Believable had been blown out of all proportion. A complete misunderstanding, nothing more. HEFFER was right. Society was fatphobic. Harriet would not tolerate this prejudice, this unfair treatment, anymore. She'd had enough. Sitting alone in the gloomy cell, she decided some hard lessons needed to be taught to the narrow-minded, narrow-waisted community. She, Harriet Etna Hambeast, was the woman to do it. On Monday morning when Om-Believable reopened, she would pay sleazy, greasy Sandyrama and those bony, Botox bitches one final visit.

When Harriet arrived at Om-Believable at six-zero-five, the dawn sky was streaked with hues of red. It was fitting for what she had in mind. She crept along the brightly lit path and tiptoed up the steps to the porch. The police tape had been removed, and all the signs pointed to the school having resumed its normal operations. Shiva was willing after all.

The ladies' class was already in full swing and the chant 'Om' resounded down the sparsely furnished hallway. Evidently, the Persian rug could not be salvaged by the industrial cleaners. The sliding doors at the end of the corridor were wide open. Harriet could see Sandyrama and his class seated in the lotus position with their eyes closed. The room was packed and full of new faces. She crept along the corridor, snuck up to each animal cage, and slid across the bolt. No one noticed her, and the animals were dozing. It was easier than she had anticipated. She pulled the snakes from their tanks and flung them into the middle of the room.

Eyes sprang open as she tipped over a wicker basket filled with scorpions. She watched with bated breath as the Komodo dragon scurried out of its enclosure toward a dark-haired beauty slowly emerging from her meditative trance. The sleeping baboon jolted awake and burst from its cage as Harriet flung open the steel door. The screeching beast launched itself into the air and wrapped its limbs around a woman's head. Blood-curdling screams of horror broke through the stunned silence. Harriet quietly slipped into the baboon's empty cage and held the door shut.

The enraged animal embraced the suffocating woman, fucking her in the mouth whilst its powerful jaws chomped on her skull. The sharp fangs pierced the bone, and the baboon tore off the top of her cranium. A muffled scream escaped from the trapped woman. The baboon scooped out her exposed brain as if it were a strawberry blancmange and shoved the pink, glutinous mass into its salivating mouth. Harriet smirked as the monkey sucked out all the contents of the dead woman's head.

From the safety of her cage, Harriet grinned and gnawed on a half-eaten corn cob she'd discovered amongst the debris on the floor. She peered down the corridor where a horde of terrified ladies scrambled for the exit. An army of scorpions with raised tails blocked their path. The wailing women hopped and tottered over the threshold, clutching at the bare soles of their stinging feet. Scorpions hung from their toes like baubles on a Christmas tree.

The baboon sprang onto another woman, grabbed her under her chin, and tore her jaw off. It beat the detached, bony structure against the ground in a show of dominance then used it to bludgeon an older, slightly built lady to death.

The room smelled like an abattoir, and flies buzzed in through the open front door. Harriet batted away the insects trying to share the tidbits she'd unearthed from the baboon's cage. A wheezing woman crawled along the polished floor toward her. The Burmese python's muscular body was coiled tightly around her torso. Harriet cringed as the woman's ribs cracked with a sound like a truck backfiring, and bone shards thrust through her chest. The woman sucked in gasps of air between vomiting up strings of slimy internal organs. Harriet's eyes widened as she looked at the glistening heap steaming on the bloody floor beside the cage.

A young woman with a lotus tattoo on her forearm stood frozen in front of the black mamba. Several scorpions scurried over her shoulders and through her braided hair. A soft whimper escaped her clenched lips and triggered the snake. It darted forward and sunk its fangs into her cunt. Harriet gawked and instinctively placed a protective hand over her own crotch as the woman's pussy ballooned to the size of a bowling ball, stretching her tight yoga pants and leaking venom and pus down her shaking legs.

A handicapped woman with a gimpy leg tripped over the huge black mamba. Harriet had seen a television horror show on snakes. The reptiles don't have ears. The bones in the jaw pick up vibrations and send signals to the brain. Sure enough, the snake had been waiting and reared up its coffin-shaped head. Its black mouth gaped open, and it struck the crippled woman in the face. She wailed, and her trembling hands pulled at the slender, scaly body. The black mamba had hooked itself onto her eye, and as she yanked, her eyeball slipped out of its socket. She tugged at the serpent until the optic nerve snapped. The black mamba swallowed the severed eyeball and struck the groaning woman in the bloody, gaping cavity until its head was buried deeply within hers.

A loud crash drew Harriet's attention to a drama unfolding in the corridor. The few who'd managed to scurry over the scorpions were greeted by the monstrous Komodo dragon blocking the door to the garden. It snapped its enormous jaws at the closest female's kneecap. As the paralytic toxins in its drool worked their venomous magic, the mortally wounded woman collapsed to the ground, shrieking in pain. The dragon clamped onto her chest and ripped off both her tits. She hugged her torn t-shirt to herself and, paralysed with shock and poison, watched the majestic reptile gulp down each breast whole. The last two remaining women tried to vault over its scaly back. The dragon snapped at their crotches and smashed the bones in their legs with a lash of its burly tail. Harriet quivered with excitement. She never imagined revenge would be so sweetly satisfying.

Sandyrama crawled out from under a folding table and bolted for the door. Harriet bellowed and threw open the cage door to intercept his escape. The heavy metal smacked the yoga master squarely in the face. He staggered and flung his hands over his smashed nose and burst lips. Harriet charged from the cage and kicked the hissing black mamba in his direction. He screamed in agony as the snake buried its curved fangs deep into his calf muscle and then slithered up his body. The blood-spattered baboon ignored the snake uncoiling from Sandyrama's face and pounced. The animal humped against the yogi, releasing several spurts of monkey jizz over his silk trousers as Sandyrama dragged himself past the Komodo dragon. The giant lizard hissed and regurgitated the remnants of the female yoga practitioners. Harriet was hot on his heels. Sandyrama stumbled out of the front door and down the porch steps. The baboon relinquished its grip on him, scaled a wooden fence, and scampered down the street, jumping along on the bonnets and roofs of parked cars as it grunted to itself.

His face distended and bloody from numerous lethal snake bites, Sandyrama clasped his hands together in prayer. "P-p-please, H-h-Harriet, h-h-have m-m-mercy. W-w-we c-c-can t-t-talk a-a-about t-t-this. I-I-I'll m-m-make y-y-you t-t-thin." She looked deep into his blue eyes shot with unhealthy colours. Once she'd seen in them the dreams and hopes of a slimmer future, but now they contained only false promises.

Harriet shook her head. "Fat is beautiful!" She shoulder-charged Sandyrama and sent him splashing into the piranha pond. The ravenous fish swarmed over him and attacked immediately. Their razor-sharp teeth tore at his flesh. Sandyrama screamed as his partially devoured arm, dangling frayed tendons, flailed at the edge of the pond. His bare chest heaved to the surface. The skin and muscle tissue had been stripped off, and the fish were tucking into his juicy innards. The feeding frenzy churned up scraps of human meat and silk fabric to the surface of the seething, bloody water. Harriet sneered at the bare ribs jutting through the ripples. "Channel that, you silk-pyjama-wearing cunt," she muttered.

Harriet stepped onto the path and watched the python and black mamba slink from the porch into the undergrowth. A flurry of scorpions followed, scuttling down the steps and disappearing under a large log. Rays of pale light spread through the trees and across dew-soaked grass. A strange thumping came from behind Harriet. The Komodo dragon had wandered from the building and was flicking out its forked tongue as it lumbered over to a patch of dirt under a cabbage tree and lay down. Harriet turned her face to the warmth of the rising sun and once again thought how peaceful it was here. She shuffled out onto the quiet street and mulled over what to have for breakfast. She decided to celebrate and reward herself with a family-size egg muffin, complete with extra sausages and several rashers of bacon. Dr Fothergill-Brown would likely be preparing to go to his office about now. Harriet wondered whether he'd ever seen a Komodo dragon up close before.

DEMONECTOMY

The rhythmic throb of his granite cock jerked Jonathan from a troubled sleep. He groaned in pain. Peering under the blanket, his eyes locked onto the silhouette of his engorged phallus standing to attention. It pulsed in the darkness, making the tops of his thighs quiver erratically and disturbing his blanket. His bollocks appeared, big and blue, two weighty meatballs encased in a bag of sweaty, wrinkled skin. He pinched his thumb and forefinger together and delicately peeled the nut sack away from his leg.

The pre-dawn boner wasn't the type you got when you needed to hop out of bed in the night to take a mega piss. This was much more serious. Possibly terminal. Jonathan's prick was a starved beast in its death throes. For the last year, his member had subsisted on a regular diet of *Fake Taxi* and *Backroom Casting Couch* video clips and Corrina's discarded, crusty panties languishing in a basket of untouched dirty laundry. The thought of his girlfriend's stained gussets caused his cock to slap his belly.

It wasn't that Corrina didn't want to fuck him. She couldn't, not since her *friend* had arrived. The contours of her ample bosom rose and fell as she sighed. Oh my god, those juicy tits. Mountainous triple E delights that defied gravity and protruded from her chest waiting to be fondled and sucked. His trembling hand reached across and tweaked a strawberry-sized nipple. It was hard. Jonathan stuffed his face into the pillow to muffle his whimpers. He needed more than a cheap feel. He needed to ram his pulsing love bone inside Corrina's snatch and fill her with at least a litre of molten spunk, otherwise he would go crazy. At

Jonathan's touch, Corrina's breathing deepened. Did she want him to slide his flesh pole inside her? She must be as desperate to ride his fat cock as he was to impale her with it.

Corrina was a heavy sleeper, but unfortunately her *friend* wasn't. He never slept as far as Jonathan could tell. Still, this act of forced pussy deprivation had gone on long enough. Sex used to be the best while Corrina slept, and Jonathan was prepared to take the risk. The early morning light filtered through the curtains. She rolled over, and he pulled the blanket back. Corrina's luscious, thick rump nestled inches away from him. That was all the invitation Jonathan needed. Tugging down her Spongebob Squarepants pyjama bottoms, he exposed her soft, peachy ass.

Jonathan rubbed two fingers over her labia. They were squishy and moist like freshly chewed bubble gum. The tips of his digits found the sinkhole between her beefy folds, and he plunged his fingers into the squelchy slit. A fart screamed from Corrina's fanny. Bugsycat and Malcolmcat bounded off the end of the bed and darted from the room. "Oh my god, your cunt is so fucking creamy, Corrina. Do you want my prick inside you, huh? Do you want me to drown your cervix with my seed, you nasty little girl?"

Corrina snored in reply.

"How about it, babygirl? Maybe get the head nice and wet in your fuck tunnel before I have a bash at finally stretching your virgin asshole." Jonathan stroked his cock with his free hand as he worked a third, then a fourth finger, inside Corrina's ripe gash. He shovelled her sopping cunt until he was buried up to his knuckles. Perhaps Corrina's *friend* was gone at last!

Jonathan gasped in pleasure as he dipped his cock into the steaming fuckhole. His nob bunted against something hard and hot. "Piss off, you rapist," Corrina's hole snarled.

Jonathan jerked his penis back in fright. Fuck. Juglorok was still in there. "Come on, man, I really need this," he begged. "Internet porn just isn't doing it for me anymore. I need some real cunt."

"I said get lost, you pervert. It's not going to happen. Do you think I want you roughing me up and jizzing all over me?" Juglorok said.

One more day of blue balls and a swollen erection was sure to kill Jonathan. He was already gulping down anti-depressants. A couple of thrusts was all he wanted – needed – to empty his enlarged testicles. Corrina let out a protracted snore. He dipped his prick inside again. Howling, he yanked it straight back out, eyes wide and watering as he inspected the bloody teeth marks adorning his purple crown. "Fucking twat! You nearly bit my cock off. Have you no sympathy? I'm desperate."

"Serves you right," Juglorok said.

"You cock-blocking bastard," Jonathan moaned. He punched Corrina in the pussy with a splattering straight right.

"What the fuck, Jonathan?" Corrina sat bolt upright. Damp tendrils of purple-dyed hair stuck to her face. She looked around the bedroom with bleary eyes and saw Jonathan cradling his cock as if it were a premature baby. "You've been trying to fuck me while I've been asleep again, haven't you?"

Jonathan gulped. He averted his eyes, ashamed of himself. "No, I mean, not really... well, yes, but only until that demon nearly severed my cock with its teeth." He glowered at Corrina's plump pussy. A skinny, red arm shot out from her silken flaps and gave him the middle finger. Jonathan lunged at the hand, but he was too slow. His fist closed around a tuft of purple pubic hair. Corrina shrieked. She lashed out with her feet, kicking Jonathan off his side of the bed. He thudded onto his bare ass, legs akimbo. His cock drooped downward subsiding into his thick, musky carpet of sodden pubes. It came to rest on his huge balls. "I can't live like this, Corrina. I need your pussy. If I don't have it soon, I'm going to die," he sobbed.

The two cats crept back into the room and began sniffing around Jonathan's slick, semi-hard cock. Corrina slid onto the floor beside her weeping boyfriend and rubbed soothing circles across his hunched back. "Hush, sweetie. I've got an idea."

Jonathan lifted his head up and looked at Corrina. "We do anal until Juglorok decides to finally fuck off back to hell?" he said hopefully.

"Eww, no," Corrina replied. "You know how much I don't like the thought of having a willy up my bum."

Juglorok sniggered from inside his vaginal lair.

"I was reading about a girl who had a similar problem to me. She got a demonectomy," Corrina continued.

"A what?" Jonathan and Juglorok asked in unison.

57

Corrina picked up Bugsycat and stroked his head. He purred. "It's like an exorcism, but for pussies."

Jonathan scratched his head. "How will having Bugsycat and Malcolmcat exorcised help with our sex life?"

Corrina shook her head, dumbfounded by Jonathan's stupidity. "No, you idiot. Not pussy cats. Pussies. Vaginas. The only problem is it's very expensive."

"How much will it cost?" Jonathan pushed Malcolmcat's head away from his scrotum.

"Twelve thousand pounds."

"We can't afford that." Jonathan started to cry again.

"I know, I've thought about that too. Listen. I found a site on the dark web where people are paid to do real sick shit. Maybe we could raise the money that way."

Jonathan fondled his greying chin hair. "Hmmm, I'm not sure, Corrina. I wouldn't have to fuck kids or anything, would I? I'd hate for my parents to watch it and think I was a kiddy fiddler."

Juglorok guffawed. "I'd even give you all the money to see that!"

"No way, nothing like that," Corrina said. Her eyes lowered to her pussy. Jonathan's eyes followed her gaze. "I did have something in mind we could do though."

A gentle breeze blew across the briny surf of the English coast, ruffling Jonathan's straggly hair as he stared at the public toilets next to the car park. Any other time he would be happy to be at the beach on a sweltering hot morning, but not today. The sun's rays felt like a furnace on the back of his neck as soon as the breeze dissipated. Sweat poured off him though he'd only been standing outside the small, grey, concrete building no more than five minutes.

He wiped his brow with a clammy hand. His eyes itched and burned from another sleepless night. Could he go through with it? What was being asked of him was some really twisted shit. Images of Corrina's deliciously meaty pussy flashed in his mind, and his cock stirred, sending a dull ache down his thighs. There was no way he could spend another day consumed by thoughts of how to get his cock into her hole without being severely injured by a demon. He could barely function. All he could think about was pussy. If he didn't get some soon, he was afraid he'd cheat on Corrina, and she deserved better than that. Besides, he had no money for a high-class escort. He'd have to take his chances with the toothless, fish-smelling slags down the local pub who would offer up their mottled, loose cunts in exchange for a pack of twenty Benson & Hedges.

A steady stream of sunblock-coated bodies wrapped in beach towels made their way past him into the women's entrance of the building. "Are you going to stand here all day?" Corrina asked. "I've got a human centipede diorama I have to finish for a book review by this afternoon." She was wearing a red micro bikini that barely covered her breasts and gave her the most awesome camel toe Jonathan had ever seen.

He glared at her. "I'm waiting for things to quieten down. It's so damn busy."

"Of course it is, Jonathan. We don't get much sun. As soon as it comes out, people are going to hit the beach." Corrina adjusted her hips and a piece of boiled beef poked out the side of her briefs. "Just get it done already."

"Yeah, go on, Jonny boy," Juglorok urged. "Though I don't reckon you got big enough balls to go through with it. Maybe another year of no pussy will sort that out for you."

Corrina was right. The task wasn't going to get any easier the longer he delayed. Twelve grand wasn't going to magically appear either. Jonathan huffed. Why couldn't his girlfriend have had a genie that granted wishes living in her cunt instead of a fucking demon? "Okay." He sucked in a deep breath and followed an elderly woman with leathery, wrinkled skin into the toilet block. Corrina followed behind, iPhone in hand. It was stifling hot inside, and the air was heavy with a heady ambrosia of shit and stale piss. Fat, buzzing flies crawled over every tiled and porcelain surface. Jonathan's eyebrows shot up. He was shocked by how disgusting the women's public toilets were in comparison to the gents'. The elderly woman joined a queue of flushed, fidgety females. In front of her, a mother and her young daughter waited for one of the stalls to become vacant. The mother hugged her daughter closer when she spotted the agitated man dripping perspiration.

The ancient biddy turned around and eyed Jonathan up and down. "You're not meant to be in here. You're a man," Granny said.

"This is the twenty-first century. I identify as a woman, so fuck off, you old bigot," he growled back at her. There was a lot of straining and the rustling of toilet paper going on behind the locked stalls. Jonathan needed to get this over and done with as soon as possible. Someone was bound to call the police the longer he lingered. "Ready to livestream, Corrina?" he asked.

She gave him a thumbs up before holding her phone to eye level. Jonathan shoulder barged the nearest cubicle door and landed in the lap of a teenage girl who was taking a dump while checking her bejewelled Samsung Galaxy. She screamed and bolted for the door, her bikini briefs around her ankles and a half-emerged turd protruding from her asshole. A huge, smoking, brown log was curled around the bowl like a sleeping snake in a shallow, yellow pool. Jonathan wasn't here for that though. His eyes darted toward the feminine hygiene bin squatted in the corner. Specks of dried shit and blood dotted its white, plastic sides. Jonathan snatched up the bin and clasped it to his chest. He hurried out of the stall.

The toilets had quickly emptied except for Corrina who was filming his every move. Jonathan squinted in the blinding sunlight and blundered past the small crowd gathered around the building's entrance. Some people were consoling the hysterical girl whose shit he'd interrupted. From the oily bosom of a fat woman with skin like a leather suitcase, the girl pointed at Jonathan and shouted "That's the paedo! He tried to rape me when I was having a poo."

Two burly men scowled at Jonathan and began to move toward him. Heckles and shouts erupted from the plethora of hostile faces. Now that he had everyone's attention, Jonathan pulled the lid off the sanitary bin. The two wannabe heroes stopped in their tracks, unsure of whether the disturbed man was going to throw the contents of the receptacle at them. The pungent, rotten, fermented herring stink made Jonathan's head snap back and his eyes roll in their sockets.

The bin was a cesspool of unfertilised eggs and uterus tissue. Dirty tampons and sanitary napkins were stuffed in up to the rim, the top layer wet and slimy from fresh vaginal secretions. Jonathan jammed his hand into the container and pulled out clumps of tampons and pads and tossed them into the air. Many were coated in a dense, membranous, yoghurt-like substance. Some were soiled in streaks of flaky shit. Bloated flies walked lazily across the banquet of filth until Jonathan swatted them away. The bin hadn't been emptied in weeks; the metallic, bacterial stench seared Jonathan's nostrils and wafted toward the shocked horde who stood frozen, wide-eyed, and with mouths agape.

"This guy's crazy," a woman shouted. "Somebody do something. Stop him!" All the men rubbed their necks and looked away, unsure of what to do. The crowd edged back as sticky tampons and pads rained down and splatted around them. When the container was empty, only a dark brown gloop sloshed around in the bottom. A thick pudding skin dotted with dead insects and long, black, curly pubes floated on the surface. A few onlookers were already retching from the horrendous pong that permeated the air.

A couple of bronzed Adonises wearing no more than a pair of budgie smugglers watched, bemused, at the front of the gathered crowd. "Hey, Sean, why don't you stop this weirdo, eh?"

"Fuck off, Simon," Sean replied. He took a swig from a large can of San Miguel. "I've seen Netflix shows about dodgy cunts like him. Obviously, he's a nutter. Best thing to do is to let him get on with it."

"I should write a book about the mad bastard," Simon replied. "People would fucking love it."

Jonathan held the foul-smelling receptacle above his head. His stomach grumbled in protest at what he was about to do. All the spectators who hadn't run away or fainted went deadly silent, unable to tear their eyes away from the morbid spectacle. He cracked his jaw open and gradually tilted the container upside down. The menstrual treacle slowly slid to the edge of the bin and dangled over the side, right above his quaking mouth. The crowd gasped as if they were watching a daredevil circus performance. "Hurry up, Jonathan, stop fooling around. Those dolls won't attach their asses themselves," Corrina growled.

"Yeah, come on, pusscake! Show me what Corrina's vagina is worth," Juglorok shouted from the wet well inside her bikini briefs.

The brown slurry filled his mouth and covered his features like a grotesque face mask. He wiped the clotted residue out of his stinging eyes. Jonathan tried to gulp down the congealed, tangy clumps, but his body resisted. The semi-solid balls of cervical mucus and pussy blood were too thick and chunky to swallow without chewing first. Jonathan bit into a gooey ball. The stringy clot erupted in his mouth, and the juice dribbled down his chin. Loose pubes tickled his throat as he swallowed the rancid mass of stagnant cunt jam. "That's good, Jonathan, that's good," Corrina shouted.

"Mother of god," an anonymous voice screamed. "Won't somebody call the police?"

"I agree," Joglurok said. "Let's get this nasty pervert banged up pronto for disturbing the peace."

Jonathan was pretty sure it wasn't illegal to drink tampon juice, but he couldn't, and nor did he want to, hang around to find out. Summoning all his willpower, he ate more of the fetid vaginal waste. His hand spooned into the swampy muck at the very bottom of the bin that was crusty and black with age. He scooped up a handful of yeast residue and stuffed it hungrily into his mouth. The acrid concoction slithered down his gullet like a giant oyster. As soon as the fishy, copper discharge hit his stomach, his gut contracted. He tried to keep his meal down, but it rose up his throat, and squirted violently from his nose and mouth. He puked out an endless river of period blood all over himself. Corrina's iPhone was in Jonathan's face when his crimson vomit splashed onto her enormous tits.

People everywhere were puking on the sandy ground. Women and children were wailing and crying. The crowd scattered as he pushed his way through the clamour, and with Corrina, he sprinted for his car and jumped inside. He dripped blood and mucus on the upholstery and smeared it on the steering wheel. "How was that?" he croaked. "Reckon we can make twelve thousand pounds from that video?" His cock throbbed eagerly at the thought of finally being buried balls-deep in Corrina. After a year of no full-on penetration, her pussy must have become tighter than most women's assholes.

The demon's voice rose from between Corrina's legs. "You disgusting pig," it said despondently. "I can't believe you actually did that."

"Haha!" Jonathan smirked, displaying teeth stained a mixture of glorious red and a shit brown. "Fuck you, demon! Fuck you! The cunt is mine! Ha!" He waved the middle finger of both hands at Corrina's groin.

Corrina bit her bottom lip. "Erm, Jonathan?" she whispered. Her voice was sheepish.

"What is it, my love?"

"I'm sorry to tell you this, but I forgot to press the record button."

An inhuman cackle emanated from between Corrina's legs and cut through the noise of police sirens that gradually got louder as Jonathan sucked on his teeth and his stiffy dwindled in his pants.

MUNGING

The swing doors crash open, and I splutter into my steaming pot noodle. Cobie, the orderly, pushes a bariatric gurney the size of a semi-trailer towards us. It's the third fatty this week. When will they learn that eating Krispy Creme donuts as if they're fruit loops is hazardous to their health?

"I've got a ripe one for you, boys." Cobie's face splits into a wide grin. Barry, my supervisor, raises his eyes from his well-thumbed copy of *Doggy Dicks in Teenage Chicks* magazine. "Darlene here's been soaking in the Yarra River for a week," Cobie says, wheeling the gurney up to the desk.

Barry flings down his magazine and levers himself out of his chair.

"The officer reported she was still on her mobility scooter when a fisherman located her at the bottom of the river. The preliminary investigation indicates she drove straight off the towpath into the water. The toxicology report is pending, and the relatives are coming in to identify her," Cobie reads from his clipboard.

"Mobility scooter, you say?" Barry's eyes light up. He unzips the body bag halfway. A pair of ginormous breasts, with areola the circumference of a luncheon meat roll, burst out of the bag. The bloated face inside has boiled-egg eyes and swollen, purple lips. The flesh is the color of a honeydew melon.

The smell hits me, and my half-chewed mouthful of noodles spews out and splats onto the table. The corpse reeks of rancid garbage water that a hobo must have used to bathe in. "What the fuck?" I gag and press my hand to my mouth. Drool and soy sauce dribble between my fingers and dangle from my chin. In my two years working at the city morgue, I've never smelled anything this foul.

"You could have waited until I left, Barry," Cobie says and edges back toward the door.

"Pussy!" Barry yanks down the zipper. A belly like a slimy river boulder bulges out followed by a bloated pubic mound. Viscous, black fluid seeps from her cavernous cunt and asshole. Barry sticks his finger in Darlene's asshole up to his knuckle. He stirs the digit around in the squelchy orifice and withdraws it dripping with strands of black slime. "Gooey!"

Cobie stumbles through the doors. I hear several dry-heaves and snorts before Cobie's dinner splashes over the floor and sprays the walls. Barry and I laugh. We've seen worse things seeping out of corpses' holes. He unzips the bag all the way and stares at the squashy legs with collars of fat hanging over the knees and ankles. "This is the one I've been waiting for." He bends over her and rubs his hands together."

"You want me to fuck her?" I ask.

"Yeah, and then I've got something that will really blow our viewer's minds."

I swallow nervously. Barry's a really sick fucker and a legend on the dark web for his creative content in the world of necrophilia. One time he made me use a stillborn baby as a dildo, and another time he forced me to fuck a surgically removed colon, riddled with cancerous tumours, that he'd retrieved from a medical waste bin. His videos get millions of views and glowing five-star reviews. I can't imagine what kind of weirdos like to watch this warped shit.

I just agree with whatever Barry tells me to do because our content earns crazy money. There's no way I want this gravy train to end, ever. At this rate, I'll be retired by the end of the year and fucking corpses in some morgue in the Bahamas.

"Do you know what munging is?" Barry asks, wiggling his eyebrows.

"Nope." Barry is a depository of revolting terms.

He shoots me a mischievous smile. "You're in for a real treat then, Maverick. Our subscribers are going to go wild when they see what you are about to pull off."

"What do I need to do?" I wipe my sticky hands down the front of my turquoise scrubs and edge over to the gurney for a closer look at the body.

"It's simple. You fuck Darlene here in the shitter and then wrap your lips around her asshole. That's when I jump onto her belly. The impact will force out a tsunami of jizz, putrified guts, and liquid faeces straight down your gullet."

My eyes dart to the girl's leaking orifices. There's a puddle of fetid, brown and green fluid that looks like pond scum beneath her huge buttocks. Given how bloated her belly is, a shitload more is festering inside. I love fucking corpses, but the thought of guzzling down what's inside them revolts me. "You're kidding, right?" I say, hoping that Barry is pranking me.

"Nah, this video is going to make us a small fortune and turn you into a big star. You'll be renowned among degenerate perverts the world over for performing the grossest, most diabolical shit that no one with a shred of decency or self-respect would ever contemplate doing. Our audience will confirm you are truly and disgustingly disturbed and totally batshit crazy. They won't be able to get enough. Man, our ratings will go through the roof."

Barry knows how to sweet talk me, but I'm not convinced. "I could jump on her belly," I suggest.

"You're the main attraction, my friend. People want to see a young stud like you, not an old codger like me getting down and dirty with the deceased."

He's right about me being a young stud. At six foot three, with chiselled abs and a nine-inch cock, I have quite the fan club. Granted, not all my fans are female, but that's fine by me. I'm all about diversity and inclusivity in the world of necrophilia.

Barry peels the body bag from Darlene. She's repulsive. Her body's so swollen that the skin has split, and spongy, yellow blobs of subcutaneous fat protrude from the gaps. "You get yourself hard, and I'll fetch a ladder and the camera," Barry says.

I strip off my top to showcase the prized abs, drop my pants, and kick off my shoes. My cock is stuck to my inner thigh. I peel it off, and my meat dangles lifelessly between my legs as if it's a salami hanging in the window of a delicatessen. With a firm grip, I give it a tug. I shut my eyes and focus on breathing. Images of sexy, dead women pass before the inside of my eyelids, Kim Kardashian's mangled remains spread-eagled on a railway track,

Ariana Grande slammed full force by an oncoming bus, and Selena Gomez taking it in the face with a shotgun blast.

"Whoa, nice work, buck." I peek out from squinted eyes. My tool is a rod of iron. Barry gives me the thumbs up from across the room, a folded ladder under one arm and the video camera attached to a tripod slung over his other shoulder. "Ready to get your dick wet, stud?"

"Fucking oath."

"Okay, spread her legs and fuck her pussy first," Barry says, glancing through the eyepiece.

I spread Darlene's legs. Her cunt looks like a possum that has been steamrolled after bingeing at an all-you-can-eat buffet. I clamber on top of the dead girl, cockslap her cunt, and rub my girthy, purple head between her green labia. My hands grip the sides of the gurney, and I inch inside her furry sea cave. "Yeah, baby, you're just like a virgin." Dead chicks' holes are always tight. It's got something to do with the decomposition process.

"Show her a bit of tenderness for our female viewers, dreamboat. Give her a kiss. With tongue!" Barry knows how to increase our profits, so I don't argue. Early retirement, I remind myself. Think of white, sandy beaches, coconut rum, and basking all day in the warmth of a brilliant sun. I press my mouth to hers and slip my tongue between her rubbery, lifeless lips. Her tongue's covered in pieces of grit and wet bark and feels like a dead fish as I tussle with it.

I thrust my cock in deep and slam into something solid. My dick bends and sharp nails pierce my nob. I howl in agony and fear and jerk backward. A long, slimy black thing's fastened to the end of my dick. "Jesus! It's got my cock. Get the bastard off me." I scream and spin in circles, thrashing my shaft around.

"It's just an eel. Hold still." Barry lunges at the head, and his fingers pry open the jaws. He holds it out at arm's length and admires the gleaming snake-like fish. "Wow, it's a beauty. You should be proud of catching this one." The eel twists and lashes at him, and he flings it across the morgue.

I stare at the deep puncture marks on my nob. Droplets of blood pitter-patter over my feet. Barry wipes his hands on a handkerchief and passes it to me. "Here, give it a dab." What a mood dampener. My cock being savaged by an eel was the last thing I expected. The fucking thing must have wriggled into her cunt cave when she was in the river. Business like again, Barry resumes his position behind the camera. I need a few minutes to get my stiffy back. I close my eyes and return to my dead celebrity fantasies until I'm hard again.

"Time for some wholesome ass fuckery," Barry says.

I press my bleeding cock head against Darlene's asshole and inch inside. It feels good, like a shitty asshole the day after its owner has binged on Taco Bell. I thrust hard. Loud gurgles rumble from the depths of Darlene's stomach and a thick, black goo squirts over my balls and thighs. The gurney wobbles precariously beneath us as I pound the dead meat.

"Yeah, baby girl, fucking take my dick!" I groan. The boiled-egg eyes stare up at me. This is so hot. I'm going to blow. I gasp as the pleasure pulses along my shaft. "Oh, God, I'm cuuummmmiiing!" My balls tighten as I pump hot seed into the decomposing guts.

Barry fiddles with the camera, adjusts the ladder, and climbs up. He perches on top like a hairy, medieval gargoyle. "Come on, stud, what are you waiting for? Slap your lips around her asshole."

I use the blood-speckled handkerchief to dab at the frothing and bubbling hole. Dragging in a deep breath, I stretch my mouth over the misshapen orifice. Fuck a corpse in the ass and the gape doesn't go away. My tongue burrows into the well of slurry seeping out of her. The bitter taste makes my eyes water.

"On three." Barry stands up. "One, two." He teeters near the edge. "Three. Cannonball!" Barry launches off the ladder with his knees tucked into his chest and a gleeful grin plastered on his face. He lands dead centre onto the corpse and Darlene's belly deflates. A tidal wave of squelchy, liquid innards gushes down my throat and spurts from my nose.

"Suck it up, megastar!" Barry says, bouncing up and down on the sunken torso.

I gulp down the foul concoction, swallowing hard to shift the coagulated clumps lodged in my throat. The flood eases to a trickle, and I slump between Darlene's pillowy thighs. A belch rumbles up from my distended gut. Regurgitated muck fills my mouth. Suddenly I don't feel so good and projectile vomit all over myself, Barry, and the dead girl.

Barry tries to shield himself from the barrage of pinky, brown puke, but it's too late. His bewildered expression is barely visible beneath the frothy gunk dripping from his face.

"Sorry, Barry." I struggle not to laugh and give him back his soggy handkerchief.

"You sick fuckers," Cobie utters from the doorway.

Still heaving, I look up as the orderly stands in front of the swing doors. Behind him are three strangers. One is dressed in a police uniform. The man and woman next to the officer are pale and bleary-eyed. Cobie steps to the side. "Allow me to introduce Mr and Mrs Williams, the parents of the deceased. They've come to identify the body of their daughter." The woman bursts into strangled sobs and collapses into the man's arms.

I sneeze out a strand of black slime. Behind me, I hear the rhythmic slap of the eel on the tiled floor.

Wuflu

The warm rays of Californian sunshine beamed through the window panes directly onto Obama's ebony fur. He was curled up in the crevice between Caitlin's thighs, next to a quietly snoring Hillary. Caitlin stroked his soft body. The large Persian cat's hair was silky and hot. Caitlin reclined in the window seat, pursed her lips onto the end of a straw, and took a sip of her mochaccino before quickly pulling her medical mask back down over her mouth.

She was on her first coffee break of the morning. It'd taken a few weeks to settle into the routine of working from home, but Caitlin had adjusted to it without too much trouble. Now, two months into the lockdown, virtual meetings and lone working was the new normal. At least she had her two cats to keep her company, even though they spent most of the day lounging over various bits of living room furniture fast asleep. Caitlin was employed as the Senior Misinformation and Harassment Officer at Klegg's Biscuits Corporation. As head of the human resources department, she shouldered the responsibility of ensuring the staff successfully transitioned to working from home during the lockdown.

According to the most recent update on MSNBC news, the spread of COVID in the United States was soaring on a relentless upwards trajectory. The governor of California urged people to stay off the streets for fear they could drop dead and injure, or even kill, any in their close proximity. How long would they have to stay locked up in their houses? No one could say. Caitlin's first task of the day involved scolding employees for various professional transgressions. She mentally reviewed the list of offences so far this week. Neil Smiggins had refused to wear a face mask during a virtual meeting, so she forwarded his personal details and home address to the PEDO squad. The special branch of *Police to Eliminate Deadly Outbreaks* was established by government specifically to control any 'unfavourable situations' that may arise from the enforced lockdown. After the riots in the Capital, it was deemed a necessary requirement to have on hand an authority ready to deal with unruly members of the public who took issue with the orders they were expected to follow.

Abdullah Jihad was given only a verbal warning for not controlling his twelve-year-old wife. During a board meeting over Skype, Mrs Jihad had run amok in the background, stripped off her burqa, and acted like an insolent child by watching cartoons with the television volume on full. Caitlin conceded to his request for mercy because Abdullah promised to beat the girl for her shameful behaviour. Tabitha Smith was reprimanded for snacking on a meat platter during a call that ran into the lunch hour. The meat platter triggered Alicia Pancake, a staunch vegetarian. Caitlin then informed Ted Nobless he would be issued with a two-week suspension for sniggering at a sexist joke, but not Ralph Gibson, who told it. Ralph was exempt because the incident happened on a Wednesday, one of the days in the week when he identified as Ralphine, a female.

Caitlin kneaded her temples recalling the altercation with Polly Socks. Getting her to admit her misdemeanour was like trying to nail jelly to a wall. The new admin assistant was told she couldn't wear black face during working hours, but Polly was adamant it was spray tan. Caitlin was forced to restate the official dress code in detail and advise Polly she would receive a written warning in the mail for her racist behaviour. Lastly, John Guffhard was given his marching orders for refusing Sabine Cooper's sexual advances via email, thus proving he was transphobic.

Caitlin peered out of the window of her apartment. The street below was eerily quiet. The lack of weekday bustle was one of the things she still hadn't become accustomed to. A man jogged in the park opposite the apartment block, his German shepherd keeping pace beside him. He wore an armband with a yellow star. His dog sported a similar band around one of its front legs. The state of California made it compulsory to wear the star band if you were exempt from remaining indoors at all times on the grounds of having a medical condition such as anxiety or working key jobs like nursing or policing.

"Dear God. I can't believe it. The mask isn't covering his nose," Caitlin gasped. She jumped to her feet, disturbing Hillary and Obama who bolted from the room with their fur sticking straight up. She flicked the latch on the window and pushed it open. "Pull your mask up now," she screamed at the top of her lungs. Her hand curled around the nearest plant pot on the windowsill and threw the cactus in the man's direction. She couldn't believe people out there were disregarding public safety by not wearing their masks correctly. It was bad enough some people were allowed out whilst others were not. In her mind, it should be one rule for all. No exceptions. The man waved jovially and continued jogging. The dog barked ferociously at her. "I'm reporting you to the PEDO squad," Caitlin shrieked.

She snatched up her cell phone and rang 1-800-SNITCH on speed dial. With the phone glued to her ear, she paced back and forth for thirty minutes before Jahnavi, in the Mumbai call centre, answered and recorded a detailed description of the incident. The flagrant violation of rules shocked her, and she continued to stride around the room, frowning and worrying her hair. Caitlin needed something to calm her down and return her to work mode. She selected a bottle of Chardonnay from the fridge and slumped on the couch with her crystal glass and a fresh straw.

The sunbeams had shifted from the window seat to the couch. Obama and Hillary padded into the room and hopped up onto the cushions next to her. Obama lifted his leg then proceeded to tongue his asshole and tiny cock. He didn't have any testicles because he was neutered. Hillary snuggled between Caitlin's legs and kneaded her crotch. The cat purred loudly. Caitlin didn't mind having her pussy pawed. Hillary had always done weird stuff like that since she was a kitten. The feline enjoyed collecting Caitlin's dirty underwear and dragging it under the bed. She always watched Caitlin in the shower too, blinking slowly from the doorway.

Caitlin reached for the Chardonnay. Damn, it was empty. She must have finished the entire bottle without realising it. The room was slowly spinning, and her head was light and fuzzy.

The kneading made her cunt tingle, and she wondered whether cats could be lesbians. How long was it since she'd been fucked by a man? Eight weeks? Twelve? Longer, perhaps? Time had become a blur since the start of the pandemic. She didn't hook up with office colleagues because everyone hated the HR personnel. They were viewed as the gestapo of the workplace. Instead, she used a plethora of fuck buddy apps. She wasn't interested in relationships. She wanted hot, hard, non-committal cock. At first, she'd meet guys on sites like *Horny*, *Woke and Single*, *Erect and Politically Correct*, and *Wholesome Meats*, but the men were all beta males and terrible in bed. They'd apologise after cumming on her face and seemed reluctant when she asked them to piss on her tits.

Just before the first wave of COVID struck the West Coast, she'd signed up to *DestroyMyHoles.com*, eager to be ploughed by real men. The thought of all the hammerings she'd received by males of various sizes and colours, who paid for dinner and didn't talk about their feelings, made her pussy slimy with desire. "Mmmm," Caitlin murmured. Hillary's paws felt so good. She decided to take the afternoon off, and if her boss asked why, she'd say she was feeling ill with COVID symptoms. She wanted to spend a little time with Black Jack.

The Black Jack Varicose Vein Special was under the sink in the ensuite. Caitlin lathered it with KY Jelly, stepped out of her clothes, and lay on the bed. She spread her legs, her soft thighs sticky with cunt juice. Since lockdown began, her pussy had grown hairy and unkempt from the lack of visitors. It looked like a hamster that'd been shoved through a mangle. Hillary pounced on the damp panties, sniffed at the crotch, and hauled the fragrant catch under the bed. Caitlin moaned as her greedy cunt sucked in the ten-inch vibrator. She shoved the big, black cock in and out of her fuckhole with ever increasing speed. "Yes, yes," she moaned, arching her back and hips to meet her thrusts. The vibrations made her teeth rattle. Breathing was difficult in her mask, and her face became increasingly hot and flushed, but who needed oxygen when smashing your own cunt felt this good?

Caitlin's crotch was about to explode when the vibrator stopped. She grumbled as she pulled it out of her sopping snatch. A long tightrope of vaginal snot linked the greasy, domed silicone head to the quivering, yawning hole. "What the heck?" She examined the black dick then shook it. "It must be the bloody batteries." Her oily fingers fumbled around in the bedside drawers flinging out condoms, tissues, lip balm, but no batteries. "Damn it," she huffed. There was no way she could get herself off without the earth-moving vibrations of Black Jack. The pandemic had seriously affected the postal services. Any batteries she ordered from Amazon today wouldn't arrive until the end of the week at the earliest. Fat chance she could wait that long. She slammed the vibrator onto the bed. Bloody hell, what was she going to do?

Hillary jumped up on the bed, sniffed the vibrator, and licked the tip. Caitlin's eyebrow shot up and her pussy tingled. She tottered through to the kitchen and fetched a sachet of the cats' favourite food from the cupboard. "Here, kitties, din dins are ready." Hillary and Obama purred and rubbed against her shins as she lured them back to the bedroom and onto the bed. She ripped open the sachet with her teeth and squeezed the jelly meat over her gash. Her fingers prodded small chunks of gourmet chicken inside herself. Caitlin bit her bottom lip as she worked the last dollops of her cats' dinner over her bulbous clit. Hillary and Obama jumped on the bed, their eyes fixed on the sloppy meal. "Eat Mommy's pussy, darlings," she moaned, smearing the meaty paste deeper into her slit. Hillary didn't hesitate and licked hungrily at the meat burrowed in the sopping wet cunt.

Obama hung back and sniffed the air. Caitlin held out a dirty finger to entice him, and he edged forward, licked it clean, then joined his sister at the bush. "Oh, oh, my, that feels so good!" She writhed under their rough, attentive tongues, pushed her boobs up, and tongue-flicked her nipples. As Hillary worked her clit, Obama tugged and nibbled at the protruding flesh flaps, mistaking them for morsels of chicken. Hillary moved down and lapped up the gravy-coloured pussy froth oozing out of her squirming owner while Obama sleepily groomed his paws. "Oh! You're so dirty, Hillary!" Caitlin gripped the side of the bed and thrust her hips in the cat's flat face. Facial fur stuck to her pussy folds as Hillary tongue-fucked the last remnants of jelly meat out of the gaping cavity.

On the brink of an orgasm, Caitlin slammed her legs together and almost squashed Hillary's head. "Reeooww!" Hillary was trapped between her owner's thighs and going nuts. Caitlin jerked her legs open, and the two cats scrambled to escape the room while her heart pounded against her ribs, and a large, soggy pool of brown jelly and cunt slime formed under her ass. Her thighs tingled and stung from the crisscrossed, bright red scratch marks. *Maybe it'd be better to order some batteries after all,* she thought.

When Saturday rolled around, Caitlin stayed by the window and watched the Teletubby-esque figures waddle down the street in their hazmat suits. They fumigated the sidewalks and the homeless people who slept on them. A white PEDO van crawled alongside on the deserted road. Sirens flashed and long, blue shadows were cast onto the walls of the nearby buildings. When the van stopped occasionally, the rear doors burst open, and three or four hazmat-clad bodies hopped out to pick up the semi-conscious vagrants off the ground and bundle them into the back of the vehicle. Caitlin smirked and waved cheerily as the van sped off.

A cat slunk through the iron railings of the park and sniffed a plastic hamburger wrapper lying in the gutter. A large population of stray cats had always lived in the park. The poor creatures were starving now people no longer ate their lunch or picnicked there. Caitlin could only imagine what a chowder of ravenous cats would do to her pussy. Her knees weakened, but she quickly shook the thought from her mind. Having her snatch eaten out by two Persian cats was a one-off, a moment of lunacy never to be spoken about. It wouldn't happen again.

Her cell phone beeped. She looked at the text message. Tim was on his way. Tim was a guy she let fuck her in the ass over a dumpster behind a Dunkin' Donuts shop just before the outbreak wreaked havoc on her sex life. He was also a delivery driver who'd started a side gig selling a gamut of much sought after products he'd stolen from the Amazon warehouse. Toilet paper, hand sanitizer, batteries, Tim was the guy who could get the scarce stuff for you at the right price.

Coronavirus was on the rise. An official statement that morning had declared the country was in a state of emergency. The government demanded no one leave their premises whatsoever, unless you either worked for Amazon or UPS. "To alleviate increasing tension during this trying time and to keep up morale, people must be able to continue to shop online," the president reasoned in his press conference. "Spending money on stuff is the foundation on which this great country was built. For the sake of the nation's mental health, Jeff Bezos is firmly behind the government's plan to allow couriers to perform their deliveries unimpeded as long as they take proper precautions to limit the risk of spreading COVID. They will be given top priority for the new Coronavirus vaccine, as well as be expected to wear masks and sanitize their hands after touching all surfaces."

Though it wasn't required of the general public, Caitlin felt the wearing of hazmat suits, even inside homes, should be mandatory. Dressed in her favourite vibrant yellow suit, she flicked her attention between the PEDOs outside cleaning up the street and the MSNBC news broadcast blaring from the television.

The door buzzer announced Tim's arrival. Caitlin hurried to the front door in her hazmat suit, her rubber boots squeaking on the parquet flooring. She was naked underneath and already wet for cock. She thumbed the buzzer to let Tim into the building, and opened her door in anticipation. Through the thick lining of her face cover, she strained to hear him ascend the winding stairs leading to her floor.

"Hello, Tim," Caitlin said through her respirator as he stood in front of her, his face half hidden by a medical mask and his gloved hands clutching a cardboard box.

"Erm, hi. Here's all the items you wanted. Two dozen packs of double A batteries, wet wipes…" He held the box out at arms' length for Caitlin to take it. "That'll be the usual hundred and fifty bucks, please."

"I was thinking we could work out a different form of payment this time, Tim." Caitlin winked. She tried to lean against the door frame and push her tits out, but the hazmat suit was big and awkward, and she ended up stumbling backward into the hallway. "We can discuss it in the bedroom. Hurry up. Close the door."

"Erm, okay then," Tim said, licking his lips. He scurried into the apartment, following Caitlin to the bedroom.

"Do you have protection?" Caitlin said.

"You mean condoms?"

"No, I mean, are you vaccinated against COVID?"

"Erm, yeah, I guess so," Tim said, stroking the growing lump over the top of his pants. Caitlin's eyes were drawn to the bulge, and she instantly remembered Tim was especially girthy. He pulled off his gloves and mask quick as lightning.

"What do you think you're doing?" Caitlin asked.

"I thought we were going to fuck," Tim said.

"We are, but you are aware we are in the middle of a pandemic, right?"

"Yeah."

"It's a deadly disease, Tim. It could in all probability kill off most of the world's population. Blatant disregard of the rules to keep the Coronavirus from spreading is very... very... un-American, Tim." The desire to ride a real cock was suddenly overshadowed by Tim's show of indifference. She could feel her pussy getting as dry as a Christmas turkey.

Tim lifted his cap and scratched his bald head. "Erm, okay."

Caitlin noticed the flurry of skin flakes drift away from his reddened scalp. *I'm sure itchiness and excessive scratching is a symptom of Coronavirus*, she thought. "Just take the money and leave my premises immediately. Stand over in the corner and don't touch anything whilst I get my purse."

As the months in lockdown passed by, Caitlin's supply of batteries dwindled. Black Jack, held together by parcel tape, barely resembled a vibrator anymore. Hillary and Obama refused to eat their dinner unless it was served in a cat dish, and Caitlin was forced to back away by at least six feet once she'd placed their bowls of food on the ground. She couldn't concentrate on her work, so she cleaned out the drinks' cabinet and switched back and forth between MSNBC and CNN instead. Her mind wandered from the news; she'd stare longingly at the two cats licking themselves with their sexy, papillated tongues. They looked up, glowered at her with distrust as if they knew what she was thinking, then resumed their grooming.

Caitlin snivelled, feeling sorry for herself. The prospect of an indefinite lockdown with two grumpy cats, no alcohol, and a barely functional vibrator depressed her. She had to do something about it, but didn't know what. Her brooding was interrupted by the high-pitched wails of hungry felines drifting in through the open window. "Poor cats," she said. Hillary and Obama stared blankly at her. "They must be starving." Juice dribbled out the folds of her cunt and soaked her panties.

She waited until midnight before she dashed across the empty street to the park, wearing her hazmat suit and carrying a box of cat biscuits. "Here, puss, puss," she whispered and shook the box of biscuits. She scanned the area for any PEDO vans on night patrol, but there was not a soul in sight. Her whispers were answered by frantic meows. Within seconds several malnourished cats squeezed through the fence. Caitlin sprinkled a few biscuits on the sidewalk. Dozens of patchy, bony felines gobbled up the treats, then whined for more. They rubbed themselves against Caitlin's rubber outfit. She smiled at their display of affection. Scattering a trail of biscuits into her apartment building, she led the horde of mangy cats up the stairs, through her front door, and finally into the bedroom. Hillary and Obama arched their backs and hissed. Caitlin scooped them up from the bed and flung them into the wardrobe.

The strays circled her feet as she slipped out of the hazmat suit and grabbed the extra-large tin of tuna from the beside table. She yanked the pull tab and the pong of tuna surged up her nostrils. The cats yowled and stretched up on their hind legs frantic to reach the fish she was smearing over her breasts, thighs, and ass. Caitlin leapt onto the bed and poured the briny liquid over her cunt and poked the pieces of fish into her vagina and anus.

A huge tomcat with a scarred face, frayed ears, and a missing eye peered cautiously over the edge of bed. More motley faces with twitching whiskers joined him. They were a filthy bunch, and she might get some horrible pussy disease, but she didn't care. It wouldn't be the deadly Coronavirus. MSNBC didn't mention anything about felines contracting COVID. The president never said stay away from stray cats in his press conference. She was so wet between her legs chunks of tuna floated down her thighs on a river of pussy juice. The tomcat leapt onto the bed. He sniffed the tuna tentatively. Caitlin parted her cunt lips so the big cat could get a good look at the meat poking out of her hole. "Come on, you know you want it," Caitlin beckoned.

He lapped the fish out of her snatch with gusto. The other stray cats jumped up and joined him. They licked at the flakes of fish all over her body, their tongues rough but gentle. Caitlin moaned and shivered in ecstasy. Some of the cats worked her nipples, circling them with their tongues to clean up the tuna-flavoured brine. The tomcat pressed his face against her wild, sticky bush and stuck his spiny tongue deep inside her pussy, lapping at her vaginal walls. Strays rimmed her asshole, eager to get at the tuna from the puckered well. Cats swarmed over her. There must have been at least forty, all scabby and flea-bitten. They covered every inch of space on the bed, and the air vibrated with their purrs. Their tongues ravished Caitlin's flesh, desperate to soak up any missed morsels of tuna.

Caitlin moved her hips in little circles and moaned. This was incredible. The big tomcat must have done this before. "Yes, yes, fuck me, you wild beast," she yelled. The tomcat growled and pushed deeper until half his head was sucked into her cunt. His claws dug trenches into her pale skin. Cats licked at the fresh blood weeping from the cuts in her inner thighs. Caitlin cried out.

She was going to cum. Her pussy erupted. A tsunami of bliss flooded through her body. The cats tore bigger gashes in the flesh of her thighs whilst others scrambled over her naked body and raked her with their sharp claws to get at the warm blood spilling from the wounds.

A sharp pain stabbed inside Caitlin's cunt as the tomcat sunk his teeth into her tender vaginal canal. She tried to rise, but a blanket of cats anchored her to the bed. "Hillary! Obama! Help me!" she cried, before her mouth was smothered by a stray cat's foul-smelling, mite-infested anus. The Persian cats whined feebly from inside the wardrobe. The horde gnawed and scratched; the scent of blood sent them into a feeding frenzy. Sharp fangs pierced her lips. The coppery blood surged into her mouth and filled up her throat. Caitlin clasped her hands around the tomcat. Only his hind legs and tail remained outside of her cunt. He wriggled and kicked at her as he chewed hungrily on her cervix.

Claws dug into her abdomen, splitting open the skin to reveal the gleam of pink innards and yellow fat. The cats burrowed inside her, hissing and fighting over the juicy organs. Caitlin looked down at her mangled body. The strays dragged coils of guts across the bed and feasted on them. Some gnawed at her stomach. The organ burst and splatted the cats in green bile.

As her life slipped away and the strays gorged, she heard a MSNBC newscaster's voice speaking slowly and deliberately from the television in the sitting room. His voice wavered as he solemnly delivered the current COVID update. "Latest figures showing the number of deaths due to Coronavirus indicate the disease continues to spread throughout the country with no sign of slowing… the president is due to give a press conference shortly… stay safe in your homes, lock your doors… it's a disease the likes of which we've never seen before… there's death everywhere… may God bless the United States of America… here's Janette with the weather report."

SCISSORS

The doorbell chimes out a few bars of Lou Reed's 'Walk on the Wild Side.' I throw down my *Women's Only* magazine and look out of the lounge window. Gavin, the postie, whistles and waves to me. My heart punches against my ribcage. Today I am expecting a letter that will change my life forever. Before opening the door, I pause in front of the full-length, hallway mirror. My pink, silk kimono is open at the front, and I cup my hands under my bra to perk up my double Ds before flicking up the ends of my wig and unlocking the door.

Gavin smiles and I return his friendly greeting. I think he fancies me. Glancing over his shoulder, I see my elderly neighbour, Mr Brownsword, peering over the top of his hedge, licking and smacking his lips. He must be doing some early morning pruning. The shrubbery he's standing behind shakes. I know he has onset Parkinson's disease, but he must have taken a turn for the worse lately. "What have you got for me today, Gavin?"

"Bunch of letters, for now." He winks and hands over a bundle of mail secured with a rubber band. "And this one which needs to be signed for." He holds the white envelope in front of me. The blue NHS stamp in the top corner leaps out at me, and my Adam's apple bobs up and down in my throat. This is it. I freeze for a second before seizing the letter and yanking it out of Gavin's grasp.

"Thanks," I grunt. Gavin's always ready with a stream of small talk, but right now I'm keen to get rid of him and find out what the letter from the NHS says. I notice his eyes glance down at my cantaloupe-sized breasts.

"I was wondering if you'd fancy a dri—"

"—No thank you, Gavin. Sorry, I'm busy all this week." He's a nice guy and all, but he's just not my type. I'm pretty sure he's mildly retarded. He also has a withered hand, and I wouldn't feel comfortable if it touched me. I close the door firmly and run into the lounge.

Ensconcing myself on the sofa, I take a deep breath and tear open the envelope. My eyes race over the single, typed sheet.

Dear Miss Daphne Potter,

After careful consideration of your request for gender reassignment surgery, we regret to inform you that your application has been denied. Due to budgetary restraints and the information you have supplied, the operation has been deemed non-essential. Should you still wish to have gender reassignment surgery, it will be at your own expense.

Yours faithfully,
Mary Hope
Senior Gender Reassignment Specialist

My face reddens. "If I could afford it, I would." The air catches in my chest and I can't breathe. I screw up the letter and fling the paper ball to the ground. "Transphobic cunts." I sink back into the sofa where a Himalayan cat lies sprawled on the armrest. I never anticipated they'd say no, otherwise I wouldn't have spent my life savings on these new tits. Society is meant to be progressive and supportive of marginalised groups. It isn't fair. The National Health Service pays for fatties to have gastric sleeves fitted all the time to stop them from stuffing themselves with cakes and pies. Unlike gender, it's their choice to eat too much and become obese. It's not my fault I was born in the wrong body.

Now I'm stuck with a cock the NHS refuses to remove. "What am I going to do, Mr Wigglebutt?" The cat opens a sleepy eye, sees I don't have any food, and closes it again. I eye the bottle of gin on the shelf of the drinks' cabinet and get up to pour myself a triple with a splash of tonic. I drain it in two gulps, and pour another, and then another, until the bottle is half empty.

My kimono has risen up past the top of my thighs and I stare down at my crotch. The familiar sight of the huge bulge in my lace panties greets me. My penis is enormous and unladylike. Tucking doesn't work. All it does is make it appear as if I have a severe case of haemorrhoids. I pull my willy out and glare at it. It's floppy, meaty, and crisscrossed with thick, salmon-coloured scars. Whenever I'm upset, I always take it out on Colin the Cock. "I hate you." Colin stares blankly. The pee hole stretches in a long, thin line, indifferent to my hostility. "I never asked to have you. You just grew, and you shouldn't have." I throttle him tightly. His head swells and flushes bright purple. It hurts but feels good too. I stomp through to the kitchen, still choking Colin, and rifle through the drawers searching for the scissors I use to cut up meat and poultry. I flop back on the sofa, clasping the scissors and gin bottle, and scowl down at Colin who has gone numb.

"Why can't you just fuck off, Colin?" The dick hole stares at me like the great Eye of Sauron. "Stop looking at me. Stop judging me." I twist the tip of the scissors into the urethral opening. "Everything is your fault." I dig the scissor blades in deeper until blood bubbles out of the hole and runs down the veiny shaft onto my leg. It hurts like a son of a bitch. Usually, it feels therapeutic, but today it's not working.

Frustrated, I shake Colin violently then punch him in the head until he's throbbing and swollen. I rake the scissors across the tender, purple flesh again and again. I still feel nothing but hurt and anguish. "Fuck you, Colin," I scream in anger.

I open the scissors wider and press the blades to the base of my cock. "I should cut you off, you filthy worm. Then I can get the cunt I deserve." I take another shot of gin straight from the bottle and snap the scissors shut. A searing flash of pain shoots from my groin to my toes. I peer down at Colin. He's lying nonchalantly on a bed of pubic hair. My crotch is warm and wet, and my nose catches a strong whiff of ammonia. I poke Colin with the scissors. He rolls off the thatch of hair and dangles from the edge of the sofa, suspended in the air by a few strings of flesh. "Oh my God, what have I done?" I whimper. I can't leave him hanging there like a hooked fish. Since I've gone this far, I'll have to remove everything. After another large swig from the bottle, I snip at the tissue between my legs until what's left is a bloody mess of flappy skin. Pinching my fingers, I peel the nut sac away from my groin and Colin follows still connected to it. The mound of raw meat plops to the floor. Colin and his bag of balls lie between my feet.

My heart thumps aggressively in my chest, and my cock stump spurts blood several inches into the air. An intense burning sensation travels down my quivering thighs, but I don't care about the pain as much as the blood. Why's it bleeding so much? Colin wasn't even erect. "Fuck, what am I going to do?" I haul myself up. The blood sprays over Mr Wigglebutt's beautiful, white coat. He hisses and runs from the room, leaving crimson pawprints on the carpet. I press a cushion against my pulsating stump to staunch the flow, but the blood continues to pump and soak through the cushion onto the carpet. If I don't stem the flow soon, I'm a dead woman.

I remember watching the movie, *Rambo*, when I was a little girl. In one scene he cauterises a wound with a burning branch. A trail of blood follows me to the kitchen. I turn on the stove element. It glows red in seconds. My wound can't reach, even when I rip off my panties, hitch my leg up onto the countertop, and thrust my hips downwards. I'm forced to climb up and squat over the top of the stove, careful not to roast my asshole.

Blood splatters onto the element and hisses and smokes. I lower my stump onto the hot plate, scream in pain, and jerk back. Blood still oozes from the wound, and I press my stub back onto the glowing element. After counting to five, I tear my charred flesh from the hotplate and half fall to the floor. I writhe on the cool tiles, sobbing and retching from the stench of burnt, hairy meat.

The jets of blood have stopped. My stump is covered with a black crust, and my thighs are streaked with dark, coagulating blood. I'm going to have to call an ambulance to rush me to the hospital, but first I must ensure some overzealous, genius surgeon can't reattach what I've detached. A pulse pounds behind my eyeballs and blood dribbles down my throat from where I've bitten through my lip. I'm close to passing out, but my butchered off-cuts must be disposed of. This might be my one chance of scoring a free pussy.

I scoop up Colin and the testicles from the floor. He looks small and sad in my cupped hands. He's covered in blood and it seeps out both ends. His helmet has gone from purple to grey. I'd drop him in the blender if I could and put him out of his misery, but I don't own one. As much as I despise the prick, the least I can do is treat him like a departed pet and bury him in the garden. I turn off the stove and lurch out of the back door and across the lawn with him and his package clutched in my hand. I'm not much of a gardener and the flowers have long ago been choked to death by weeds, but I find a pleasant spot under the shade of an apple tree. I fall on my hands and knees and start to dig Colin's grave. The soil is soft from last night's shower. I lower the cock and balls into the hole and pile the damp soil over them.

"Nice kimono," a voice croaks behind me. I turn my head and see Mr Brownsword on the other side of the fence, ogling me. "But I bet you've got something much nicer under it." He coughs up a wad of green phlegm and brushes it onto his shirt. "How about you pull it up and show me? Grandpa wants to see your lovely, round bottom. I haven't seen a derrière as juicy as yours since I was stationed in France during the war." I've got no time for this lecherous, old creep. The best course of action will be to do what he wants. That should make the horny bastard piss off. I pat down the earth and sprinkle a few leaves over the small mound.

I lift my hands from the ground and slowly pull up the silky fabric, pausing midway to slide it from side to side over my bottom and give him a smirk over my raised shoulder. His raspy breath increases. I wiggle my ass and draw the kimono up to my waist. My hands caress my buttocks and disappear into my ass crack. I part my cheeks to give him a good eyeful of my barbecued bits and perform a few more wiggles. "What in God's name is THAT?"

"Do you like what you see?" I'm feeling woozy and my speech is slurred. Mr Brownsword stutters in shock. "By the way, you couldn't do me a favour and phone for an ambulance?" The world fades to black and my face hits the dirt.

My eyelids flutter open. I am lying on my lounge sofa with an IV-line dangling above me. A female paramedic, whose name badge says she's Sara, kneels between my legs and tends to my groin. Her partner, Ryan, a young male, slumps against the wall and stares at me with wide-eyed horror. "How long have I been unconscious?" I ask, groggily. The cooked stub of my severed cock is a furnace of agony.

Sara glances at her watch. "A little over six minutes has elapsed from the time we received the call to finding you prone in the back garden and transporting you inside." She nods at the cannula in my arm. "I've given you something for the pain. It'll kick in shortly, then we'll get you to hospital. "Did you do this to yourself?"

"Yes," I reply.

Sara shakes her head and proceeds to slather my wound with a cream that stings to fuckery and then dress it with bandages. "Where's your penis now, sir?" She observes me from between my legs.

"It's ma'am," I correct her. "I put it in the blender and then I drank it."

"Oh my God." the male ambo sprays his shoes with puke and runs from the room.

Sara finishes treating me and then coaxes her partner back to help lower me onto a stretcher. I am rushed to hospital with lights flashing and sirens blaring.

A hospital psychiatrist evaluates me whilst I'm recovering in bed. She deems my actions to be related to a gender identity crisis. The hospital is very supportive and grants me a vagina, free of charge. I'm bumped to the top of the waiting list, and before I know it, I'm being told the surgery is a success. Within a week, I'm out of hospital, a new woman.

My cis female friend, Susan, has been around to feed Mr Wigglebutt. She left me a note stuck to the fridge saying she'd cleaned up the paramedic's vomit and my blood on the carpet, but she was unable to clean Mr Wigglebutt properly due to her own blood loss from severe feline lacerations. Mr Wigglebutt is waiting for me at the front door and wants more food. After I feed him, I head to my bedroom for my thrice-daily vaginal dilation routine. I lie on the bed with a pillow under my hips and ease off the pad taped over my raw, puffy pussy. The specialist nurse gave me a kit and five vaginal dilators from toothpick size to sword size. I have to work my way through the range until I can accommodate a colossal cock. The sword size is not as big as Colin, though. My willy was a whopper, and in a way, I was really proud of him. I don't want to poke anything into my new opening. My vagina already feels as if it's been fucked with a broken beer bottle, but needs must prevail. If I don't follow instructions, my new pussy hole will shrink to the size of a belly button and be just as useful.

Mr Wigglebutt jumps on the bed after he's finished his tuna and pads over to investigate. His eyes are wide with curiosity as I part my newly acquired labia and inspect my shiny, pink clitoris. He sniffs at my snatch and tries to lick it. I shove him away. The surgeon told me the sexual pleasure from sensitivity will come after the healing, but right now the smallest dilator feels like a flaming battering ram. Now for the hygiene bit. The nurse gave me a powerpoint presentation on how to clean all my folds.

By the evening, I am exhausted after repeating my routine a couple more times, and I collapse into bed. My sleep is riddled with dark dreams and menacing shadows tapping on the window. When I wake in the morning and draw the curtains, *LET ME IN* has been written in dried blood on the exterior of the glass. It must have been Mr Brownsword. It wouldn't be the first time I've caught him up a ladder, peering through my windows. I clean off the scrawl, but the words continue to nag at me as I go about my day. My pussy's very fat and swollen as if I've used a vagina pump. Dilation is really painful, but I grit my teeth and get through it. By early evening, I'm shattered again and ready to call it a day. I check the house is secure in case the pervert next door tries to come back during the night. I let Mr Wigglebutt out the front door even though he can use his cat flap, and stagger off to bed.

Rays of sunlight beam through the flimsy curtains and wake me. The hands on my bedside alarm clock point to ten o'clock. Dirt is smeared all over my blanket and Mr Wigglebutt sits by my pillow with what looks like a bald-headed, decomposed rat in his mouth. The cat's white face is smeared in dark brown streaks. I shriek and spring out of bed. Mr Wigglebutt drops his prey onto my pillow and purrs, awaiting my praise and affection. What the hell? The rat has balls instead of legs. I gasp as it dawns on me that I'm not looking at a dead rodent, but at a severed penis and testicles. Mr Wigglebutt has exhumed Colin and brought him to me as a gift. The cock is bloated and smells like spoiled meat. "Bad Mr Wigglebutt," I growl.

I fetch a pair of rubber gloves and a black bin bag, then scoop up the putrid mess resting on my pillow. Touching Colin gives me the creeps. He's overripe and his body undulates. If I grasp him too tightly and he bursts, I'll be showered with maggots. The testicles have distended to the size of tennis balls. A layer of slimy scrotum skin is in the midst of sloughing off, and the sac is full of little holes where creepy crawlies have gnawed through. I stuff him into the bin bag and tie the ends into a double knot. I carry Colin at arm's length to the wheelie bin and drop him inside. Mr Wigglebutt or any of the local wildlife won't be able to get him in there, but any bin raider rummaging through my rubbish will get one hell of a fright. I go inside and change all my bedding.

My first visitors arrive soon after for a post-op party, but I'm not really in the mood to entertain guests. They don't take no for an answer when I try to cancel, so I'm forced to spend the day feigning everything is alright, that I'm not in a lot of pain, and seeing a decayed Colin hasn't affected me emotionally. He looked so pathetic, all rotten and dishevelled, and I was the one who did it to him. I have to excuse myself after lunch to dilate my vagina. When I return to the lounge, everyone is still there, giggling and making jokes about me sneaking off to masturbate. I pretend to laugh. In the late afternoon, I finally manage to get rid of my visitors by telling them I feel unwell and need to rest. After they leave, guilt washes over me. I'm usually a social person, and my friends didn't deserve to be dismissed. I should be ecstatic. Colin's gone and I have a cunt, a neat one no less, and not one of those overfilled kebab-looking monstrosities. But I'm miserable, and I sob into my pillow until I fall asleep.

I'm woken up in the night by blood-curdling screeching from a catfight. I fear it's Mr Wigglebutt and rush outside and call him. He doesn't come, and I return to my bed. He doesn't wake me in the morning either as he usually does. My panic levels rise when I can't find him anywhere in the house. I search for him outside and discover him on the grass near my bedroom window. His jaws gape open, and his body is all twisted and misshapen as if something has brutalised him from the inside. I wrap him in his favourite blanket and place him in a hole near to where I buried Colin. The rest of the day is spent in vaginal dilation and weeping. The phone rings on and off, but I don't want to speak to anyone. I draw the curtains closed and ignore the doorbell when Gavin arrives to deliver the mail.

That night I'm startled awake by the clattering of the cat flap. For a moment I think it's Mr Wigglebutt. Tears stream over my cheeks when I remember he's dead and buried under the apple tree. Maybe it's a neighbourhood cat or a rat? I've had rat problems before. That's why I got Mr Wigglebutt in the first place. I lie in the darkness and listen intently.

The sliver of light from the landing widens as my bedroom door creaks open. I sit bolt upright and grip my nightgown over my breasts. "Who's there?" I croak. A shadow moves from the doorway and something scuttles across the floor. It pulls itself up the side of the bed. I'm too afraid to move. It wriggles beneath the covers and creeps toward me. A cold lump presses against my inner thighs and snuffles around my crotch. Oh God, I'm not wearing any panties. Mr Wigglebutt's absence has emboldened it, and the rodent has managed to push open the door of my room. I'm totally paralysed and freaking out.

"What the fuck?" a muffled voice says. I jerk the covers back and shriek. It's Colin. "You-you've got a... cunt," he proclaims.

Shit, I've overdone the painkillers. I'm hallucinating. I'm too stressed and experiencing a manic episode. I breathe in slowly and deeply and try to prise myself from the grip of this nightmare. This is not really happening. Panicking won't do any good. He fucking stinks though.

"Yes," I say. "I had an operation."

"You traitorous bitch. You cut me off and then replaced me with a fucking pussy. I can't believe you'd do that. Especially to a glorious specimen like me."

"I am a woman. I have complete autonomy over my body. It's my personal choice to remove a penis which conflicts with the gender I identify with." I don't believe this. I must be off my rocker. A severed cock has crawled into my bed and is lecturing me, forcing me to justify myself!

"After all you've put me through, cutting and hacking at me for years when you were depressed, and then you finally chop me off and throw me in the bin as if I'm worthless. You don't care I'm physically and mentally scarred from all the self-harm you've inflicted upon me. And to top it off, you replace me and my balls with a goddamn vagina. It's an attack on my masculinity. Oh, the shame!"

It's true. I have put Colin through hell. "Sorry," I say, meekly.

"And what about the good times? Wanking onto the gusset of your father's underwear when you were six? Jamming me through glory holes to an uncertain fate? Didn't that mean anything to you?"

"It-it did, but that was the old me. I've changed. I'm comfortable with who I am now. I don't need you anymore."

"That hurts, more than any knife or pair of scissors ever could." Colin flops down between my thighs, dejected. The cock mouth turns from a horizontal split to a downward curve. A long silence follows until Colin perks up. "This pussy of yours, is it a virgin pussy?" Colin gives my swollen lips a meaty slap that makes me wince in pain. I hadn't thought about my pussy like that before. "I guess I am a virgin, yes. I've only had vaginal dilators inside me so far."

"Good, I'd love to try virgin cunt for once. All you ever gave me was ass. Hairy, stinking man ass. I've worn more turd hats than I care to remember."

"What the fuck? No way. I'm saving myself for someone special." I try to jam my legs shut, but Colin's huge, grotesque balls block me.

"I am fucking special, and I'm going to destroy that tunnel. Return the favour for all the times you hurt me." Colin's foul, malodorous body nuzzles my vaginal entrance. "Open up, bitch. I'm going to dilate this cunt good." He thrusts himself into my pussy until only the mouldering balls remain outside me. He's much bigger than the dilators. I'm forced to expel breath every time he bunts the pit of my stomach with his bulbous head.

I thrash around and try to jerk him out by his nuts, but he's delved in deep and hammers my cunt with the ferocity of a teenage virgin with his first Fleshlight. My fingers slip and slide as I attempt to clutch the slimy, decomposing ball bag. "Stop, please!" I scream. All the surgeon's good work is being destroyed from the inside out as Colin fucks me raw. It feels as if I'm being stoked with a red-hot poker that's the same diameter as a can of Foster's. The girthy phallus pulses erratically from all the maggots feeding on the rotten shaft.

Blood seeps from my hole. My mouth gapes in agony and I go cross-eyed. Colin grunts loudly inside my crotch and then slips out of my burning pussy ring. "Aaaah, fuck yeah, that's good. The surgeon did a smashing job. Made your pussy even tighter than some assholes I've been shoved in." He slinks up my nightgown, coming to rest on my chin. The rancid odour of decay floods my nostrils. "Now, suck me, bitch. You know how much I like to be throated after I've pounded a hole. Take me nice and deep in your warm mouth."

"Fuck off," I scream. Grabbing him around the crown, I fling him across the room. He collides into the wall and slides down.

"You cow." He torpedoes through the air and slams into the side of my head. "I said take me in your slut mouth, bitch. Gag on your own cock, you whore," Colin roars as he headbutts me repeatedly in the face. I'm dazed and confused. As soon as my lips part, Colin wriggles into my mouth. The flavour sends my palate wild. He tastes of soil, blue cheese, putrefied offal, and salty piss.

His girth takes up my whole mouth. He worms in deeper, throat fucking me until my eyes water. I'm choking on rotting cock. I somehow manage to vomit out of my nose even though my airways are blocked. "Yeah, baby girl, puke all over me. I like that," Colin yells from inside my mouth. "Suck it harder, but watch your teeth. Let the drool fall onto your plastic tits. That's it, right there. I'm gonna blow! Fuuuccck!" The balls resting on my chin contract and shrivel as Colin shoots his spunk into my gob. Several spurts of sludgy, maggot-infused jism hit the back of my throat. He pulls himself out, still dribbling cum from his cock slit. "It's an insult not to swallow." My mouth is full of what feels like lumpy porridge.

"You have to chew it because dead spunk turns chunky," he says.

I shake my head. I can't do it. Colin headbutts me again and I gulp on reflex. My insides churn and growl, and the rancid baby batter comes straight back up. I spew my stomach contents all over the bedsheets. The jizz-sick is the colour of tar and smells like month-old roadkill a homeless wino has used as an ass wipe. I look down at my ravaged pussy. It's been obliterated. It looks worse than when I hacked off Colin.

The cock collapses back on the bed, flaccid. "You got to take me back. I'm dying. I need you, Dave."

"Why should I? You just raped me. And it's Daphne. I legally changed my name, remember?"

"Come on, Daphne, you've treated me like shit most of our life. It's not just about you, you know? We're a team."

I feel guilty. Not once did I consider Colin's feelings. I was selfish and never meant to hurt him. As much as I resented him stuck to my body, I shouldn't have done what I did. "How do we fix this?" I ask.

"Sew me back on."

"But you're all rotten and gross."

"I'll get better once I get some blood flow," he assures me. I limp downstairs to get a needle and thread and return to the bedroom with my sewing kit. "Mmm, keep this pussy though. I like it. Sew me over your clit so I can bend like a banana to fuck it."

I crudely sew Colin on above my pussy as he instructs. I pop a whole lot of painkillers and try to sleep. I toss and turn all through the night. My cunt bleeds from the trauma it has suffered and sticks to the bedsheets. There's a nasty red swelling spreading out from Colin as well. "You've given me an infection," I complain.

Colin hoicks up a teaspoon of black cum. "Just take some more pills. Fuck, this pussy looks so good from where I'm standing." He runs his crusty head along my sore slit and rams it in. Agonising spasms rip through me.

I gobble handfuls of pills from dawn until dusk. I can still feel the searing pain through the chemically induced haze. Colin's been buried in my pussy all day long, filling me with his necrotic seed. It hurts so much. By nightfall, not even the pills help. "Will you leave my pussy alone, Colin? I need to go to the doctor," I whine.

"Just relax. It will be better in the morning." Colin fucks me into the early hours. I pass out listening to the sound of squelching, grunts, and pussy farts.

In the morning my vagina is a festering, pus-filled, itchy mess. The stench of infection wafts out of my bright red cunt hole. Colin is lathered in yellow pus and has ballooned so much I think he's going to pop. My thighs and belly have turned an unsightly pallor mapped with spidery, dark veins. "Fuck yeah, baby girl, your pussy is scorching," Colin exclaims.

It's true, I'm running a high fever. I can barely stay awake and my nightgown and bedsheets are sweat-stained. "I need to go to the hospital," I complain.

"They'll just take me away from you," Colin says. "I'll be incinerated."

"But my vagina has gone septic." I have to get rid of Colin for good. I drag myself out of bed and stumble down the stairs towards the kitchen. Colin doesn't pay much notice. He's busy struggling to reach my pussy. He's so bloated now he can't bend very well. Opening a drawer, I take out the scissors, lurch into the lounge, and fall onto the sofa with my legs splayed.

"Mmm, you want to play too?" Colin says. His smirk becomes a scream when I flash the scissors in front of him. "What the hell are you doing?" Colin tugs against his stitches to get away, but he's rooted to my cunt. "No, don't, you bitch! Leave me alone." I sever his gangrenous head, then pick at the stitches, twisting and pulling at the shaft until he bursts, and my face is splashed in maggots and a pungent, sticky treacle. My pussy spews up a solid chunk of creamy pus in relief. The scissors drop to the floor.

I'm so sick my head falls back onto the armrest. I slip in and out of consciousness as the maggots crawl over my face and Colin's deflated, headless cock continues to try to fuck my pussy, but his thrusts are getting weaker. I think I'm dying. I think we're dying. The two of us. Together.

My name is Leo. I live on a remote research station on Stanley Island, off the coast of Tasmania, with my dad, the world-renowned, Australian marine biologist, Dr Jerald Hood. I've had a fantastic childhood, full of adventure and wonder. I wouldn't swap it for anything. Well, that was until I went through puberty. Now, instead of running riot over the island and getting myself into all kinds of mischief, all I can think about is girls and how much I want one. Chances are I won't be getting a girl anytime soon, either. Dad's going to be stationed here monitoring the aquatic wildlife for at least another five years. I have the internet, of course, and all the porn I can wank to, but it's not the same. I want to feel the flesh of a living, breathing female.

It's early morning, and though I've already rubbed two out before I even get out of bed, I decide to stretch my legs on the beach to try to take my mind off my cock's banishment to *No Pussy Island*. It doesn't work. From the windswept beach, I can see the mainland and the city on the distant horizon. All I can think about is the women on the far shore, their plump asses and pendulous breasts squeezed into micro bikinis. Bald, bronzed cunts, fat camel toes, and juicy, erect nipples that would make a man foam at the mouth. I can picture them now, luscious ladies greedily sucking and fucking big, hard cocks. The thought gives me a giant woody as rigid as a surfboard.

"Not this time, buddy," I scream at my wayward cock above the roar of the ocean. I'm sick of being a lackey to my prick. Maybe some vigorous exercise will take my mind off sex. I sprint along the soft, golden sand with the wind and salt spray stinging my face. My lungs burn, my legs turn to jelly, and my cock collapses in defeat. I breathe a sigh of relief and decide to indulge in one of my favourite boyhood pursuits - beachcombing. Some really interesting seashells wash up on Stanley Island, and I have amassed a huge collection of them at home, from rare conchs to colourful mitre shells.

Within fifteen minutes of scouring the sands, I have a smile on my face and bulges in my pockets. Dad will wax lyrical over some of the beauties I've found. I'm thinking about returning home to deposit my treasures when I spot a dolphin washed up on the beach. Foamy water laps around its tail and fins. I've seen dolphins swimming off the coastline before, but never one so close that it risks being stranded on the shore. Poor thing. Tiptoeing across the sand, I gently approach the shiny, bluish-grey body. The dolphin eyes me warily.

"It's okay, I mean you no harm," I say soothingly with my hands held out in front of me. The dolphin lies half on its side weakly flapping its tail. No injuries are visible, and I carefully check the other side. She's a girl. She squeaks as I roll her onto her tummy, and into a shallow depression beside her. I splash her with water and run a reassuring hand over her sleek skin. "There, there, you're going to be fine." She quietens down, seeming to sense I am here to help her.

She's a big girl, around four hundred kilos. There's no way I can move her by myself, but Dad will know what to do. I'm about to turn around and run back home to fetch him when the blowhole gurgles and spits out a frothy secretion. I freeze, transfixed by the sight of the bubbling orifice. It looks like a sphincter farting out a creampie in one of those anal, gangbang videos on *Pornhub*. My cock has a seizure in my pants. My left eyebrow shoots up, and I look up and down the beach. There's not a soul in sight. I've always been partial to the bigger ladies. Kimmie Buffet and Monica Mozzarella are my two favourite porn stars.

My trembling hands caress her flanks, and I slip two fingers into the blowhole, all the way up to the knuckles. She squeals, and I jerk out my fingers in fright. What am I doing? This is so fucked up. I just fingered a dolphin's blowhole. Am I really that horny and desperate? Her moist, soft insides did feel good around my digits. Really good. I sniff my fingers. They smell faintly fishy with a slight scent of ass.

Before I know it, I've slipped my leg over the dolphin. As I straddle her like a horse, I unzip my trousers and pull out my cock. Droplets of pearly precum bead the bulbous, purple head. I can't believe I'm going to do this, but I can't stop myself. The blowie looks too good not to stick my cock into, and I've been desperate to fuck something since my first pube. I scoot forward and spank the hole with my dick. The meaty, wet slaps make the veins in my shaft pulse angrily.

"You want this don't you, baby girl? You want my spam javelin deep in your filthy, tight blowhole." She cranes her head to see what I'm doing on her back. I tease my throbbing nob around the rim and then slip it in. "Oooh, fuck." I shudder. The hole's snug and hot, and envelops my tool like a friendly hand.

The dolphin lets out a high-pitched squeak as I edge myself into her until I'm balls deep. "Easy there, girl," I whisper into her earhole. My soothing words calm her. I slide my ass back and forth over her smooth skin and thrust deeply into her quivering hole. My balls smack against her body and the froth seeping from the hole lathers into a cream, coating my prick.

The animal bucks and her tail churns up the sand. I grip onto her fins and hold on for dear life. How ridiculous I must look, ass in the air and cock slamming in and out of a dolphin's blowhole. Dad would be ashamed if he saw what I was doing to this highly intelligent, friendly mammal of the sea. The tightness of the hole plus her Japanese porn star squeaks are too much for me. I can't hold back my load any longer. "I want to be a marine biologist!" I scream, as my cock erupts and I pump heavy streams of warm spunk inside the dolphin's salty gape. I roll into the shallow water and lie on my back beside her, panting. "That was incredible, baby girl." She rolls her eyes, not looking too good, and her blowhole queefs and gurgles. "I'll go and get Dad now."

I hoist up my trousers and speed off along the sand. Dad's bent over a microscope in his laboratory, examining some phlegmy substance in a petri dish. His head jerks up as I barge into the room. "A dolphin is stranded on the shore and needs our help urgently," I gasp, my chest heaving.

"Is it hurt?" he asks.

"I've checked her over, and she looks okay, but she's too heavy for me to drag back into the ocean."

"Whereabouts is she?" Dad flings off his glasses and jumps to his feet.

"In an almost straight line down from that old banksia tree. We've got to hurry, Dad." Dad claps me on the shoulder, and together we race down to the beach. The dolphin eyes us suspiciously as we approach, no doubt concerned I've brought a pal back for a threesome.

Dad circles the animal. "Good lad, you've done the right thing fetching me. She looks distressed." He squats in the sand beside her and peers into the blowhole. "She seems to be having problems breathing." His fingers probe the clogged aperture, and he scoops out a clump of congealed cum. A sudden whoosh of air escapes from the blowhole, spraying jizz in Dad's face. Dad wipes away the strands of spunk dangling from his nose and eyelids. "Oh dear, she must have a cold," he says after spitting some of my man mayo from his mouth.

A red tide of embarrassment washes over my face, and I curl my toes into the sand. "I guess so, Dad."

"Now we've cleared the spiracle we need to get her back into the water as quickly as possible. Grab the tail, son. The two of us should be strong enough to move her." Dragging a four-hundred-kilo dolphin over wet sand is no easy task, but after several minutes of heaving and grunting, we reach the shallows. Dad gives her a friendly slap, and we let her go. The dolphin flips her tail and sprays us with water before disappearing beneath the waves. "That's gratitude for you," Dad says, smiling proudly from a job well done.

I nod in agreement and go to stuff my hands into my shell-stuffed pockets. My flaccid cock is stuck to my thigh, and I wriggle around trying to peel it off without Dad noticing.

After my tryst with the dolphin, all I can think about is blowholes. I spend my days combing the beach and sailing around the coves of Stanley Island in a little dingy, but I don't see another dolphin. I think my blowhole beauty tipped off her friends and family about what I did to her.

I order an inflatable whale sex toy online. It arrives in a discrete brown box addressed to me. The damn thing is so big I nearly faint blowing it up. It's a huge disappointment when I hump it. I may just as well fuck a plastic bag. Frustrated, I resort to jerking off over blowhole videos and photos on the internet. I even join a blowhole enthusiasts' web group called *Blowhole Watches*. I ask what types of blowholes people are into fucking, and I'm kicked out of the group immediately and blocked.

I need to get off this island and get myself some real aquatic mammal hole. I apply for every job working with marine animals I can think of: marine mammal trainer, fish and game warden, aquarist. I even apply to Greenpeace. I get the same rejection letter after each application. They say I'm too young and inexperienced. One morning whilst I'm choking the bishop to reruns of the TV series *Flipper*, Dad knocks on my bedroom door. "You in there, Leo?"

"Shit," I mutter and then yell, "just a second." I tuck my cock into the waistband of my undies and pull up my bed covers. "Yeah, Dad, what's up?"

Dad pushes open the door and pokes his head around the corner. "I've got some interesting news."

Oh great, another boring lecture on the mating habits of sea anemones or some such shit. "Mmm?" I try to sound enthusiastic.

"Greenpeace called. They said a Japanese whaling fleet is chasing a pod of blue whales off the coast of Australia. If they keep to their current trajectory, they'll pass close by Stanley Island early this afternoon. I thought we'd take the boat out and see what we can do to help Greenpeace protect the pod. What do you say, son?"

My eyes light up, and a grin splits across my face. Blue whales are the BBWs of the sea. There's no mammals' blowhole I'd rather fuck. "Yeah, Dad, let's do it!" I say, pounding my fist in the air.

"Thatta boy." Dad gives me the thumbs up.

We gather up the supplies we'll need for the trip and rush down to the wharf. Our boat isn't large, only big enough to get to the mainland, but it's a beautiful day, so we should be safe on the open sea. The afternoon sun sparkles off the calm, azure waters. We head five miles offshore, and I scan the northwest horizon for the pod of whales.

The afternoon sky is changing from gold to crimson when I spot the pod being escorted by the Greenpeace vessel, *Sea Wolf*.

The Japanese whaling fleet is hot on their trail. One of the whales has broken free from the pod and is being pursued by a whaling ship. Several crew members are on deck, shouting excitedly in Japanese and pointing at their target.

"Shit, Dad. We have to help."

"It will be dangerous, son."

"I don't care. We came here to help the whales."

"I know, but we'll need to be bloody careful." Dad opens up the throttle and veers off course to shield the distressed whale. The sea's become choppy, and I'm forced to grip the side of the boat. Our small vessel is dwarfed as we draw alongside the whale. I've never seen an animal so majestic. A jet of water spouts thirty feet into the air.

My hands slip into my pants and grasp my stiffening cock. I know I shouldn't attempt what I'm about to do, but my lust for the blowie consumes me. Before I can stop myself, I say, "I'm going to climb onto the whale like in that movie, *Whale Rider*. They'll never shoot it with me on top."

Dad's body goes rigid, and he stares at me with his eyes frozen open. "Absolutely not! It's madness! The harpoonist may not even see you."

"I'm going, Dad. It's worth a try."

"It's a hell of a way to enter manhood, but I won't stop you." With one leg hoisted up onto the edge of the boat, I prepare to jump. The glistening, bubbling hole is so close, my prick dribbles like a hungry dog. I leap, then land on the whale's huge back. My fingers scrabble around the blowhole, trying to find a grip so I don't slide off and fall into the sea. "Don't let go! Hold on tight," Dad yells above the roar of the ocean.

I manage to work my pants down with one hand. My eyes sting from the constant splash of briny water, but I don't care. God, my engorged cock feels so good pressed against the sleek flesh of the blue whale. I haul myself up, and my throbbing member slips deep inside the blowhole. My prick touches only one side, but it's pulsing, warm, and wet. The sensation is electric. A deep groan rumbles from my depths. This is ecstasy. My naked ass bobs up and down as I pump the hole vigorously.

"Jesus Christ, boy. What the hell are you doing to that whale?" Dad shouts.

"Getting my end off, Dad," I shout back.

The blubbery insides of the blowhole cushion my shaft as I hammer the fuck out of the throbbing nostril. No homo sapiens' snatch could be anywhere near as good as a blue whale's blowie. Dad jumps up and down in the little boat, yelling at me to stop and get back on board. The Japanese whalers' excited babble gets more frenzied. A couple even snap photographs of me and my aquatic beauty. A large crowd of long-haired men and shaven-headed women gather on the top deck of the *Sea Wolf*. They scream angrily, boo, hiss, and throw things at me. Their hatred is palpable, but all I care about is emptying my nuts into this enormous, divine creature.

I smash the whale's hole hard and fast, edging towards a climax so intense I might pass out. As a flood of hot seed erupts from the mouth of my cock, a searing stab of pain slams into my back and knocks the wind out of me. I shoot high into the air on a jet of water and cum, then I'm yanked backwards before splashing into the cold ocean.

The pointed end of a harpoon protrudes out the middle of my chest. Dad's manic shouts become muffled as I sink to the murky depths. A cloud of blood blooms from my wound, turning the sea around me bright red. I watch the whale get smaller as it swims into the distance. My vision blurs, and I feel light as a feather. *Sorry, Dad*, I think to myself. That was one hell of a final orgasm.

The Leprechaun's Hat

I sit in the bus shelter and throw stones at the cars roaring by. The road is busy with morning commuters and the drivers can't stop, but they brandish their fists and curse me. It's a fun way to pass the time while I wait for the school bus, especially when I manage to lob one of my missiles through an open window and cause the enraged driver to swerve into the wrong lane.

I smell the old man before I notice him. The dishevelled figure sits right next to me on the bench, much too close for my liking. His beard is frizzy and unkempt, and he scratches at it with long, black claws. My eyes follow the flurry of skin flakes drifting from his face down to the weathered, grey mac riddled with holes. The dark stains on the fabric suggest he's been out in last night's rain.

He senses I'm looking at him, and he turns to face me. His mouth twists into a scowl; his eyes are red but alert. I drop the handful of stones on the ground and study a cloud in the sky that resembles an ostrich being fisted by a clown. The old man juts his neck forward and peers at me from beneath wiry eyebrows. His gaze makes me uncomfortable. I shift awkwardly to make some space between us, but he slides in closer. He reeks of fish and spoiled cabbage.

"Ma name's Mr Greentreacle, but ma friends call me Gerry," he grunts in a hollow voice.

I very much doubt Gerry has any friends. Living ones, anyway. More than likely his toxic body odour has killed them all off.

"Peter," I mutter. I try to avoid inhaling, but I wind up taking in a whiff of his ghastly stench through my nostrils and almost gag.

"Ye know me, don't ye?" He looks at me quizzically.

I ponder his question while I look up and see the ostrich swallowed by a hippopotamus.

"I've seen you about the place," I say. "Round the back of Mrs Govinder's shop, going through her dumpster."

Gerry snorts. A verdant blob of phlegm lands near my shoe.

"Aye, dat'll be me, aye." He brushes away a thick string of mucus hanging off his beard. "Dat's where ye'll be sure ta find deh best selection o' stale bread an' sundries dis side o' town," he chuckles.

"And I've seen you sleeping in the park, over on the grassy embankment near to where the dogs like to shit."

"Feckin' cunts have no respect fer a fella tryin' ta sleep. How would ye like ta wake up an' see a dog's arsehole starin' at ye o' a mornin'?"

I shrug. My eyes scan the bus timetable bolted to the shelter wall. I hope the bus comes soon. Last thing I wanted to do was spend my morning consorting with the local tramp. He fucking stinks.

"Waitin' fer deh bus ta school, are ye?"

Gerry's right in my face now. I bite my lip as I notice something crawl around in the darkness of his beard.

"I don't know." It's all I manage to utter.

"Well, ye look like deh kind o' kid who believes."

"Eh?" My brow furrows. "Believe? In what?"

"In leprechauns o' course."

My heart almost bursts out of my chest. How could Gerry know about my secret obsession with leprechauns? I've never told anyone, neither my friends nor my dad. My mum used to read me stories about them all the time before she died from cancer of the tits.

"Leprechauns! Those fat, little midgets who bury their gold under rainbows instead of putting it all into a savings account with a good annual rate of interest? Of course I believe in them."

"Dat's dem." Gerry smiles. The colour of his crooked teeth resembles my piss when I haven't had enough to drink. "It just so happens dare's one o' deh little feckers nearby in need o' yer help. Dare's deh promise o' gold innit fer ye too."

My left eyebrow shoots up. Never in my wildest dreams would I have thought I'd ever get to see a real-life leprechaun. They are very elusive fellows who don't show themselves often.

Gerry's eyes twinkle. "Silly fecker stole a wizard's hat, an' now deh hat's stuck ta his head. It's growin' by deh minute, trettenin' ta swallow him up. I'd help him maself, but only a lad believin' in leprechauns can be doin' it. D'ye reckon ye could help him?"

"Do I get his whole pot of gold if I do?" I really want to buy a Playstation 5. I've wanted one since they launched, but my dad says he won't buy me one because, as he puts it, he thinks I'm a 'lazy, useless cunt'.

Gerry rams a fingertip in his nose and scrapes out a crust of dry snot. He flicks it at a passing lady who turns up her nose at us both.

"Sounds fair," he says.

I grin at the victory. To be honest, I would have settled for a few Irish coins if it meant I got the opportunity to meet a leprechaun. I wonder if he'd allow me to take a selfie with him. Dad would be well impressed, and my friends too.

"Deh ginger prick is sulkin' in deh jacks over dare." Gerry turns and points to a public toilet behind the bus shelter. My friends and I have always avoided the public toilets. All kinds of weirdos go in there. Druggies, mostly. I'd make an exception though to get my hands on some leprechaun gold. "Come on den, laddie." He springs up and heads in the direction of the toilet block. I grab my schoolbag and follow. I have to run to keep up with the old man.

Mr Greentreacle disappears into the entrance of the squat building. I enter in after him. My head aches from the pungent ammonia stench of wino piss hanging in the air. Neon graffiti, bright pink and green, covers the walls. Several blue urinal cakes float around in a blocked-up piss trough like dead sailors fallen overboard into a frothy, golden sea. I couldn't think of a worse place to hide out if I were a leprechaun.

"Go an' wait in one o' dem stalls an' I'll fetch him fer ye," Gerry insists. He adjusts the rope belt holding up his oversized, dirty trousers and watches me intently.

I nod and go into the last stall on the left. The toilet seat is missing. A long, crusty, black turd sleeps on a soggy wad of toilet paper inside the bowl. Speckles of dry shit cling to the walls, right up to the ceiling. My stomach spasms and I feel my cornflakes rise to the back of my throat. I decide to stand. The piss-splattered, rusty hinges of the stall door beside me squeak.

"Ye still dare, laddie?" Gerry inquires as if I can somehow have gone into the stall and miraculously vanished.

"Yeah. Where's the leprechaun?" I hiss. I want to get my pot of gold, buy a Playstation, and go home. I'll tell Dad I felt ill while waiting for the bus so he'll write me a sick note.

"I'm fetchin' him fer ye." Gerry's voice drifts in from a fist-sized hole in the wall. I hear the rustle of clothes and clench my hands together in excitement.

I stare unflinchingly at the hole. There's a grunt and a miniature head squeezes through the aperture. The wizard's hat is jammed on top. I gasp. A real leprechaun! The hat is a deep blue hue, and decorated with crescent moons and shooting stars. The poor guy has an unusually long, veiny neck.

"Name's Seamus O'Doodle," the leprechaun says. "Quit yer gawkin', laddie, an' be gettin' dis here hat from off o' ma head."

My trembling hands reach out and grasp the tip of Seamus' hat. It's soft like a baby's skin. The leprechaun twitches in my clammy hand, then goes stiff. I tug at the hat, trying to dislodge it from Seamus' head. It won't budge. His pulsating neck stretches further through the hole in the wall.

"Owwie, not wiv yer hand, fer feck's sake. It's a magic hat dat belongs ta a powerful feckin' warlock from feckin' ol' Muckanaghederdauhaulia. Ye need ta use yer feckin' mouth an' suck it right off."

That seems odd, but what do I know about wizards' hats on leprechauns? I kneel down onto the sticky tiles and open wide to take Seamus into my mouth. The leprechaun squirms inside. I can feel him throb as he pushes his way past my teeth. I cough and splutter as soon as his head bunts my tonsils.

"Dat's right, laddie, suck dat feckin' hat off ma head," he cries.

Gerry wheezes loudly from the other side of the stall wall. Maybe he's struggling to hold onto Seamus. He's an old, malnourished man after all. The leprechaun works his head back and forth in my mouth. I suck hard and wrench at his neck with my hands. I hope he doesn't mind that I've coated him in my saliva. After the hat comes off, the wee guy is going to need to spend a good ten minutes under the hand dryer.

The wizard's hat tastes so salty that my eyes water. I don't like it but I keep sucking. The thought of getting that leprechaun gold consumes me. Seamus' groans ring in my ears. His head swells in my mouth. I throttle him and he moans. I know I must be hurting him, but the fucking hat just won't come off. A dull, aching pain throbs in my jaw.

"Ughh, yer a proper little vacuum cleaner, aren't ye?" he says, bemused. "Keep goin', yer gettin' dare, yer gettin' dare." Seamus' head pulses in my throat. I'm close to buying that Playstation 5. I can feel it. The leprechaun lets out a strangled cry. "Eeee, it's workin', ma lad. Get ready ta take some o' ma magic sauce." A warm, sickly, porridge-like substance blasts down my windpipe. The force hurls me back against the wall.

The leprechaun pokes out of the hole. He's no longer wearing the wizard's hat. His head looks like a purple mushroom. More thick ropes of cream-coloured magic sauce dribble out of his gawping mouth and onto the tiles.

"You fucking prick, you threw up in my mouth," I splutter. I use my sleeve to wipe the mess from my lips.

"Aye, dat I did, laddie."

"I did what you asked. Now give me my pot of gold." I screw my face up and spit on the ground. I can't get the taste of him out of my mouth.

"Not a chance, ye silly fecker. Yer goin' ta have ta catch me first, gobshite!" Seamus disappears back through the hole. I hear the pattering of little feet on the tiles as he scampers towards the toilet block entrance.

I jump up and push the door open just in time to see Gerry hobble out into the morning light. I race after him as he dashes across the road. Seamus' gleeful laughter drifts back to me. The old man and the leprechaun must be playing some sort of mean trick. Gerry clambers over a fence leading to the park. I try to cross the road but drivers zip past, left and right. I've got no chance of catching him now.

By the time I get to school, I'm sobbing with anger. I spend the day sulking at the back of the classroom, not talking to anyone. I can't believe I got duped by a tramp and his leprechaun mate. A rancid clot of magic sauce sticks to the roof of my mouth, and no matter how much I try, I can't tongue it free. My one encounter with a leprechaun and he pukes down my gullet. What a mischievous bastard.

When I get home, I burst through the front door and fling my schoolbag down the hallway. My dad is slumped on the couch, still in his dirty overalls and sipping a beer. "What's got up your ass?" he growls.

"Mr Greentreacle told me I'd get a pot of gold if I sucked a wizard's hat off a leprechaun's head," I cry. Tears stream down my reddened cheeks. "We went into the toilets next to the bus shelter and Seamus appeared through a hole in the wall. I sucked, Dad. Really hard too. The hat finally came off but he puked in my mouth instead of giving me my reward."

Dad's eyes grow wider and wider as I recount my sorrowful tale. By the time I'm finished, he's wandered over to me and gently pats my shoulder.

"That was no leprechaun, son. You sucked off a homeless man through a glory hole."

"That's not true," I shout. "I was trying to help Seamus O'Doodle!" Dad's not listening. He grabs my arm, snatches up his car keys hanging on a hook by the front door, and drags me outside. "Where we going?" I ask.

"To find that pedo and fuck him up," he replies. Dad snaps open the passenger door and flings me into the car.

We drive around the streets looking for Gerry. Dad's fuming. The veins in his neck are bulky cords, and his jaw is rigid like when he doesn't want to breathe in one of my farts. I don't know what he means by calling Gerry a 'pedo', but I'm smart enough not to ask.

It's not until dinner time when we spot the old man wrapped up in his coat, asleep on a park bench. "That's him," I yell. I stab at the pane of glass. Dad snarls. I've not seen him this angry since he caught my Uncle Barry giving me a bath when I was twelve.

"Right then," he growls. "Time to give that kiddie fiddler what for." The car squeals to a stop. Dad storms out of the car, leaving me behind. Gerry sits up and mouths "Oh feck," when he sees Dad charging towards him, his sleeves rolled up past his elbows. The tramp tries to flee but Dad tackles him onto the grass. They roll around near several piles of dog shit and a couple of perplexed joggers stop to observe the tussle.

I exit the car and wander up to the two men fighting on the ground. Dad grabs Gerry's straggly hair and slams his head into a mountain of steaming, white poop. "What did you do that for?" I bark at Gerry. His face is a mask of dog shit, and his eyes swirl around in their sockets. "You said Seamus would give me a pot of gold!"

Gerry mumbles incoherently. Dad pummels him with several hard punches to the body. "Where is he? Where's Seamus?" I demand.

Dad knees the old man in the groin. Gerry screams and I have to press my palms hard against my ears. "Oooooh, ye mean fecker," he cries. "Ye hit Seamus square on deh nose. Got him good ye did."

I pull Gerry's hands away and start to undo his coat buttons. Dad tries to stop me but I slap his arms away. "What the fuck are you doing, son?" he asks.

"Seamus has my pot of gold," I reply. "I sucked that wizard's hat off his leprechaun, and I want what's owed to me."

"Don't be a fucking idiot. I told you…"

I fling open Gerry's filthy mac. Dad and me stare at a twitching lump inside the tramp's trousers. A patch of blood blooms across his groin.

"Ye got me, laddie," Seamus croaks in a muffled voice. "Deh gold's yers. Take it an' leave us be, ye good fer nuttin' scallywag."

I tear at Gerry's rope belt and trouser buttons, eager to get at the injured leprechaun. Dad edges away from me slowly. I pull the tattered trousers down to Gerry's knees. Seamus has been bashed to a bloody pulp. "Where is it? Where's the pot of gold?" I shudder with rage.

"It's… it's…," Seamus mumbles. Gerry has passed out; his tongue lolls out the side of his mouth.

A death rattle spasms out of the leprechaun's throat. His long neck twitches and he goes still, slumped over Gerry's thigh.

I clench my fists and shake them at the darkening sky. "My gold!" I yell.

Never again will I ever trust a leprechaun.

BUNNIES

Demetri Pavlovich kicked off his muddy boots and sent them flying across the porch. He slammed the front door behind him and stormed through to the living room. An ugly red tide of colour washed over his face. A mountain of expensive bags covered the dining room table. *Bloody Marian.* His wife had been shopping again, spending money they didn't have. No doubt she had run up more debt on the emergency credit cards.

Sebastian, Demetri's severely palsied, cross-eyed son, sat in an electric wheelchair in the corner of the room. He stared at the iPad hooked onto the armrest from which emanated a series of jagged breaths and squeals. His trousers lay bunched around his ankles. One twisted hand gripped his limp, uncut cock whilst the other fondled his drooping, hairless balls. The boy's mouth hung open, and a long string of drool dangled from his chin. Demetri glared at the grotesque spectacle. His lips curled in disgust as the boy tugged on his flaccid member. As he grew more excited, Sebastian thrashed around in his chair, banging his helmet against the head support system. Inhuman noises erupted out of his throat and rose above the rhythmic *fap, fap, fap* sound emerging from between his quivering, bony thighs. Demetri turned his head away as frothy precum bubbled from the tip of Sebastian's dead dick.

Jasmine lay sprawled on a couch, her long, slender legs flung over a fancy cushion which cost Demetri more than what his parents, back in the old country, eked out for a month of groceries. Her glazed eyes continued to stare at her phone. She was oblivious to his distress and her brother's masturbation marathon. Demetri sighed. He'd left Mother Russia to raise a family in a land of hope and prosperity, but his farm was failing, and his family were behaving like the vermin plaguing his fields. "The rabbits have been at the crops again," he grumbled through tight lips.

"That's nice, Daddy." Jasmine smiled without looking up at him.

"I made some good buys in town today," Marian said as she waltzed into the room, ignoring Demetri and heading straight over to her pile of purchases. He scowled as she rummaged through one of the many Louis Vuitton bags. Jasmine snapped out of her stupor at the sound of her mother's voice.

"Did you get my iPhone, Mummy?"

"Of course, sweetie, but they only had black." Marian passed her a small bag adorned with the Apple logo.

"Aww, Mummy, you can't do anything right." Jasmine pouted. "You knew I wanted princess pink. I told you. You should have waited in the queue outside the store last night."

"Didn't you just get a new phone?" Demetri asked.

"That was last month's model, Daddy." Jasmine rolled her eyes and dropped the bag down the side of the couch without even opening it.

Demetri puffed out his cheeks and shook his head. "As I was saying, the…"

"Guh-guh-nhuh-na!" Sebastian groaned. "Guh-gah-gwahhhh! Guhhhhh!"

"What did he say, Marian?" Demetri asked.

"Oooh, fuck yeah, you dirty, little nugget bitch. Take it right up your back pussy," Marian said while still inspecting her new purchases. Sebastian's malformed hand became a blur and speckles of cock fluid flew in all directions.

"Ga-guh-ugh-gaaaa! Gaaaaa! Ugh!"

"I'm going to cum, you big-titted pillow slut," Marian translated.

Sebastian's back arched suddenly, and a wad of cum shot out in a parabola and splattered onto the carpet.

"Oh, dear. What a nasty little mess you've made, Sebby." Marian walked over and dabbed the tip of his pulsating penis with a silk handkerchief.

Demetri grimaced. "It's not natural the way you treat the boy, Marian. He's a sick pervert. He should be in a home, locked up in one of those gulags for the retarded. Back in Russia, he would have been strangled by the doctor as soon as he showed his ugly mug."

Marian cupped Sebastian's cock in her hand as if it were a dearly departed mouse and mopped up the gossamer of jizz coating his atrophied legs, shrunken and twisted from muscle wastage. "You're just expressing yourself aren't you, Sebby?"

"Gruh-huh-ha-nuh-nah," Sebastian said, one eye on his mother and the other eye swirling off in a different direction.

Marian sniggered. "You shouldn't say such things about your father, Sebby." She turned to face Demetri and eyeballed her husband with a look that could melt steel. The tall, muscular man with his solid jaw and deep-set eyes that she'd fallen in love with had become old and stringy. Angry eyes shot with unhealthy colours stared back at her from his gaunt face.

"Right, that's enough for me. I'm off. I'm going to go and poison the fucking rabbits," Demetri said.

"You can't, Daddy. That's cruel. Bunny rabbits are people too," Jasmine whined.

Demetri ground his teeth. Jasmine was a vegan. He'd had a recent swarm of those fuckers protesting on the farm when he'd kept dairy cows. Those sanctimonious assholes accosted him every time he left the house to go to work. They held up placards declaring he was a fascist and a slave owner. Some bearded freak strummed on an acoustic guitar and another bashed a tambourine while they sang soppy folk songs far into the night. Flat-chested, hairy-armpitted women poured soya milk over themselves in protest, and dreadlock-sporting, hemp-clothed men embraced each other and cried in sympathy with the plight of Demetri's cows. They eventually scattered when Demetri hosed them down with the contents of the septic tank, but not before they had converted his impressionable, teenage daughter.

"Jasmine, they're eating our vegetables and destroying our livelihood."

"I don't care. You can't kill them. It's genocide. You're just like Hitler." Jasmine held up her phone to show Demetri a picture of a fluffy bunny wearing a tuxedo. "Look how cute and innocent he is! You can't murder him. You just can't." Jasmine's eyes flooded with tears.

"They're ravenous, oversexed vermin. If I don't destroy them, then you won't be able to have any more luxuries. Kiss your new phones and designer clothes goodbye."

"Oh." Jasmine dried her eyes and flicked the image on her screen to a picture of a Hermès Birkin handbag, the cute bunnies instantly forgotten.

Before anyone could protest further, Demetri spun around and strode out of the house to his pickup truck. He hadn't cleaned it since the late nineties and the assorted trash crunched beneath his feet as he stepped inside. He drove with his fists clenched around the steering wheel. Tarseal and family homes with flowering gardens gradually replaced the dusty roads and farmlands. Trees with lush foliage swayed in the gentle breeze fragrant with the scent of blossoms. Demetri breathed deeply and relaxed his hands. By the time he drew up to the local farm supplies store, his mood had improved. Old Ed, the hunchbacked owner, was busy counting a bag of coins next to the till. He raised his watery eyes to greet Demetri as he entered through the creaky door.

"What's been happenin', young feller?" Old Ed croaked. His nose leaked snot onto his bushy, tobacco-stained moustache, and he didn't bother to wipe it away.

"The usual shit, Old Ed. The wife is maxing out the credit cards. My degenerate, spastic son jerks off all day over nugget porn, and my airhead daughter's turned into a vegan bitch. To top it all off, a plague of rabbits is destroying my crops."

Old Ed scratched his head. "What's nugget porn?"

"Girls who have no arms and legs."

"Did they fall into some farmin' equipment or such like?"

"Something like that. Anyways, I need poison to sort those fuckers out."

"You want to poison your family? I ain't sure that's totally legal, no sir."

Demetri frowned. "I'm talking about the rabbits."

"Ah, right you are, young feller. Well, just so happens I got me some special stuff in from China. Arrived last week." Old Ed turned to a shelf behind him, reached up, and took down a large, brown bottle with what looked like a rabbit with a boner on the sticker. He placed it on the counter.

Demetri cocked an eyebrow. "That's rabbit poison?" He inspected the opaque bottle, but there was only Chinese writing on the label.

"Sure is. It's on sale too. Only $19.99. There's enough pellets in there to kill a thousand rabbits. Won't spoil your crops neither. Just what you need to rid yourselves of the little blighters. Say 'Sayonara bunnies,' eh?" Old Ed guffawed, showing his almost black teeth.

"I'll take two bottles," Demetri said, handing over the cash. He smiled. Killing the bastards and saving his crops would be cheaper than he first thought. He sped home. As he drove up to the house, Demetri was greeted by the sight of Sebastian doing donuts on the driveway. His trousers were still around his ankles. Demetri's mood darkened, and he wondered if the poison worked on retards. He bet it would if he crammed enough pellets down the little turd's throat. He'd be sure to get caught though. Marian doted on her firstborn. She would demand an official investigation into his death, even though Demetri would try his hardest to convince her that people in Sebastian's condition didn't tend to live very long, and the boy most likely died from natural causes.

"Little freak," Demetri muttered. Inside the house, Jasmine was still slumped on the couch, surfing her phone. She hadn't moved since he'd left to go to the store. "I got the bait, Jazzie." He shook the bottles in front of her face and grinned.

"Whatever."

He disappeared into the kitchen and foraged through the fridge. Half of a roast and a mixed salad remained from last night's dinner. He tore off a chunk of the beef, slapped it into a bread roll, and planted himself beside Jasmine on the couch. "Want a bite, Jazzie?"

Jasmine scrunched up her face and swallowed. "You're so disgusting, Dad." Demetri laughed, spraying her with semi-masticated food. "Eww, gross. Get away from me."

Demetri was eager to get started on eradicating his furry pests. After gulping down his snack, he left his daughter to her electronic device and traipsed outside again. He extracted the corks from the bottles of rabbit poison and sprinkled the small, blue pellets copiously over his vegetable patches. The late afternoon sun hung suspended in an orange-coloured sky and cast long shadows across the verdant grass as he worked.

Sebastian groaned in the distance. He had no doubt jizzed on himself for the umpteenth time that day.

Demetri worked hard until the sky darkened and the clouds obscured the moon. He fell into bed, exhausted but with a beaming smile on his face. Marian snored loudly next to him, a sleep mask over her eyes. He dreamed of rabbits choking and shitting out their insides.

At first light, Demetri awoke, eager to witness the aftermath of a bunny apocalypse. He bounced down the stairs while still buttoning his work shirt and shot out of the front door. The day was gradually emerging. Demetri caught a glimpse of something over by the pigsty. It was Sebastian. He was watching a sow with huge tits rooting around in the muddy pen. Another pig waddled up behind the sow, nuzzled his snout into her dirty asshole, and then mounted her. Sebastian squealed louder than the pig as it got fucked. His contorted body rocked wildly in his chair, and he moaned with glee. "Mmm-guh-guh-gaaa! Ugh!" Sebastian leaned forward and allowed the thick strand of saliva to fall from his chin onto his red, raw cock. Demetri watched his son's hand switch to turbo mode now his drool had applied additional lube to his shaft. Demetri shook his head, disgusted by his offspring's behaviour. If he had stayed in Mother Russia to raise his crippled son, Sebastian would have grown up to be a valuable member of society. His organs would have been harvested and distributed equally to needy people, young and old, in the true spirit of communism.

Demetri went over to the barn and swung up onto his tractor. He toured the farm, keeping his eyes peeled for dead rabbits. Most of the pellets had been eaten, but there were no bunny corpses littering the ground, and even more of his crops had been destroyed overnight. Carrots had been uprooted and gigantic bites taken out of his lettuces and cabbages. "Fucking Chinese crap!" Demetri barked. First thing tomorrow, he'd tell Old Ed what he thought of his poison. Today there was too much work to do on the farm. He needed to check whether any of the crops were salvageable.

He drove back to the barn, despondent and angry. He passed Sebastian who had manoeuvred his electric wheelchair into the pigsty. The wheels whirred noisily, struggling to spin around in the muck. Globs of grey mud sploshed over him as he positioned himself behind the sow. Her porcine lover had left her with a gaping cunt and a dripping cream pie. The gurning boy flipped Demetri the bird as he drove past on the tractor, then he reached forward and stuck his entire fist into the sow's bloated snatch.

Demetri attached the grass cutter to the front of the tractor, climbed aboard the vehicle, and turned on the engine. Grass cutting was one of his favourite tasks because it afforded him the time and quietude to gather his bustling thoughts, as well as to reflect on his many financial worries. The day was already hot, but he didn't mind. He'd rather be outside working by himself on the farm than ensconced inside with his family.

It hadn't always been like this though. Jasmine was once his little girl who loved nothing more than to be bounced on her daddy's knee. Now she was a rabid, feminist vegan who hated meat and men. Sebastian was born retarded, but it wasn't until he discovered his penis and developed a masturbation addiction, encouraged by Marian, that he became so perverted he was nigh impossible to live with. The boy couldn't keep his hand off his nob. He was obsessed with his genitalia, and his compulsive behaviour resulted in weird, thin curls of ham-like flesh dangling from his tortured member. At night Marian would swaddle the injured phallus in soft, organic cotton after smearing it with soothing balms. Demetri had wanted Sebastian's misshapen hands amputated so he couldn't masturbate, but the doctor was appalled by the idea and threatened to report him to the authorities for child abuse. It was ridiculous. In the old country, the Kremlin would have funded the operation.

Marian's spending was out of control. The credit card bills were in excess of ten thousand bucks each month, and he struggled to keep up with them. The sex used to make it all worthwhile, but now the only action he got was a perfunctory wank that felt like a handshake from a dying man. Meanwhile, she would scroll down the pages on her phone with her free hand. Details of her wonderful purchases replaced the intimate whispers and oral sex.

All these thoughts plunged him into a deeper depression. But all was not yet lost. Maybe when Jasmine finished her feminist dance theory degree, which he'd reluctantly re-mortgaged the farm to pay for at Marian's behest, she could get a job at McDonald's. He could also pressure Marian into moving

Sebastian to a home for disabled youths, preferably one which specialised in treatment for chronic masturbators. One way or another, he'd convince her their son would be better off under the skilled care of professionals who would understand and address his specific needs.

Demetri was jerked from his reverie when the tall grass around him thrashed violently. Several heads poked up from the swaying stems. *What the hell are a pack of feral dogs doing on my farm?* Demetri wondered. The animals disappeared into the undergrowth for a moment before pouncing at the moving tractor. Their yellow teeth gnashed, their black nostrils flared, and their malevolent snarls sounded like the war cries of fauna from the deepest, darkest recesses of hell. Long ears of matted, white fur sprang from their large, broad heads. Burning, red eyes pierced into Demetri's and made his blood run ice cold. THEY WERE GIANT FUCKING RABBITS!

They bounded toward him, leaping as high as the tractor cab. One struck the window and ricocheted off the glass. Demetri looked up as another one thudded onto the roof. The thin steel of the cab buckled and grazed the top of his head. Maniacal rabbits surrounded him. Their monstrous feet thumped at the tractor, and their scrabbling claws tore at him, trying to wrench him from the vehicle. He jerked the wheel and swerved erratically across the field to escape the attacking horde. These weren't the cute, fluffy bunnies Jasmine fawned over. Gigantic incisors snapped at Demetri as he lashed out with his fist. Even more terrifying were the rabbits' ginormous erections smacking the windows. Girthy and a foot in length, they frothed and spasmed like epileptic pythons.

Demetri veered the tractor toward the house, slamming into a couple of mutant rabbits blocking his way. The huge tires crunched over their bones, and the spinning blades spewed out bloodied bunny mince and mottled fur.

A claw smashed through the cab's glass and ripped across Demetri's cheek. He yelped from the sudden bolt of pain. His foot jammed down on the accelerator, and he flung the tractor from side to side, trying to dislodge the unwanted passengers who clung to any bit of metal they could grip onto. The wind whistled through the jagged hole in the side of his face and blood seeped down into his shirt.

The tractor smashed through the pigsty. Sebastian's arm was buried up to the shoulder in the sow's cunt. His face was a mask of pig spunk and mud. The sow burst under the weight of the tires. The metal blades carved her into thick, rashers, showering the tractor and several rabbits with her gore. Sebastian was shunted along in his wheelchair before it toppled over, and tipped the squealing boy onto the ground. Demetri heard his son's bones snap beneath the wheels. A glistening mass of entrails clung to the twisted steel of his chair. The stench of raw sewerage bubbled up into his nostrils as mashed body pieces and segments of skeleton were flung from the churning wheels.

He whooped and punched his fist into the air. The tractor, out of control, slammed into the porch and threw the rabbits against the wooden panels of the house. As they scrambled around, dazed, Demetri jumped from the cab and hurled himself through the front door. He twisted the lock and wedged a chair under the doorknob before racing through the dining room and into the lounge.

Jasmine still lay on the couch, eyes glued to her phone. "We need to get the fuck out of here," Demetri roared. "The farm is overrun with killer bunnies." Black, congealing blood oozed from the torn flap of his cheek and dripped to the carpet.

"Did you forget to wear a mask when you sprayed pesticide again, Daddy?" Jasmine mocked without bothering to look up. Loud thuds shook the front door panel. Jasmine sprang upright. Her wide eyes stared at her father. "What was that? What's wrong with your face?"

"No time to explain." The door splintered open and several growling rabbits skidded across the hallway floor. Jasmine screamed and covered her eyes. Demetri grabbed his daughter's arm, yanked her off the couch, and then off her feet. She shrieked and wailed as he dragged her across the carpet before slinging her over his shoulder and lugging her upstairs to the master bedroom. Demetri slammed the door and pushed a heavy wardrobe in front of it. He slumped down, using his weight to help reinforce the door, and tried to regain his breath.

A cacophony of smashing crockery and inhuman grunts resounded up the stairs. Demetri braced himself against the wardrobe as he listened to some of the horde thunder up the steps, hop across the landing, and slam into the barricaded door.

"Do you think it will hold, Daddy?" Jasmine was curled up on the bed with her arms wrapped around her knees.

"For a while. Where the hell's your mother?"

After a hard day of fucking and shopping, Marian liked nothing better than to pamper herself by slipping into a hot tub. She stepped out of her Gia Gardoro black dress. She wasn't wearing any panties and a fine sheen of cum glistened on her pink lips. Hector, her lover and Demetri's part-time farmhand, liked it best when she didn't wear panties and when her pussy was freshly waxed, and as bald as a cancer patient. Marian slid into the perfumed water. Her triple D breasts floated to the top, and she admired her creamy satin skin and pink nipples. Marian was pleased with herself. She had looked after her body, worked out at the gym, and attended her beautician regularly. She would leave Demetri soon to be with Hector, and they would make love all day and enjoy Demetri's money after she divorced him. The thought made her nipples harden and her clit swell. She slid her hand between her legs and fondled the pink nub protruding from her slit.

The water splashed and her eyes flicked open. She thought she had fallen asleep and was in the midst of a vivid dream. Three guys in bunny suits sat in the water beside her, ogling her breasts. She covered herself with her hands and crossed her legs. *Has Jasmine told her PETA friends her father planned to poison rabbits?* Marian thought. *Have they come dressed as giant bunnies in protest and solidarity? But what the fuck are they doing in the hot tub with me?*

Before she could speak, three huge cocks popped up from the swirling water. More giant bunnies crowded into the bathroom, stroking their engorged members with razor-sharp claws. "Er, can I help you?" she asked, arching her perfectly plucked eyebrows.

The room remained silent; every pair of vermilion eyes was fixed on Marian's buoyant tits. The leering Lepus continued to fondle themselves without uttering a word. Marian slid down into the water. She wasn't averse to an impromptu gangbang with Jasmine's odd friends, but it would have been nice to follow the usual courtesies and be introduced first, instead of being surrounded by unidentified genitalia.

One of the bunnies in the hot tub leaned in and stroked her breast with its velvety paw. Shivers of pleasure coursed through her body. Marian gasped. She went limp as two furry, muscular arms hoisted her up onto the side of the tub, and a waiting cock impaled her moist, soapy cunt. The wind was knocked out of her as the throbbing prick began to beat her cervix as if it were a punching bag.

A phalanx of bunny meat crowded in around her. Marian took two in her mouth, jerked off another two with her hands, and then parted her cunt so another diamond-hard cock could slip into her fuckhole underneath the one already housed in there. She drew back from the two swollen meat sticks lodged halfway down her windpipe and screamed in ecstasy. Neither Demetri, nor Hector, nor any one of the hundred strangers she'd fucked whilst dogging over the past year had ever smashed her gash like this. *This is amazing. Nothing could top this,* Marian thought in between gagging on the two extra-large portions of throbbing dick.

"I love randy vegans," she spluttered, as one cock left her throat and was replaced by another. She worked them like a pro, barely pausing to breathe. "Which one of you bad bunnies is going to pound my backdoor then?"

Marian whimpered as she was immediately stabbed in the shitter by an overly enthusiastic rabbit. The anonymous bunny jackhammered her fartbox with demonic fury. It wasn't long before her pussy gushed all over her furry friends. "Oh my god," Marian rasped. She looked down and saw her cunt wasn't squirting vaginal fluid. Her pussy was shooting out a stream of blood. The murky, red cloud blossomed in the water, spreading outwards until it completely filled the hot tub.

As the rabbits ejaculated and withdrew their cocks from her orifices, her pussy spewed up a chowder of pinkish, white gristle. A searing pain welled up inside her guts. Marian reached under her ass and the tips of her fingers brushed the spongy lining of her prolapsed anus. Bile surged into her throat and drowned her screams. Cold and ashen, Marian slid back into the hot tub. She sank below the water as the rabbits stomped on her soft body.

Claws ripped at her skin and incisors dug deep into her flesh until they struck bone. Shredded muscles and organs floated to the surface. The rabbits lowered their mouths to the steaming liquid so their tongues could lap up the meaty soup.

Demetri watched Jasmine squirm in anguish as they listened to the ruckus in the bathroom. An eerie silence followed Marian's cries. He turned his attention to the door as an army of heavy footsteps pounded up the stairs. The wardrobe shuddered. "Daddy, what are we going to do?" Jasmine sobbed.

Demetri glanced around the room. There was nothing to defend themselves with, and the only avenue of escape was the window. They were two storeys above a concrete yard. "Help me with the mattress, Jazzie." They dragged the mattress from the bed and struggled to push it out of the window. A ferocious shove caused the wardrobe to lurch forward, and a rabbit's face appeared through the crack in the door panel. Jasmine and Demetri stood eye to eye with the enraged beast before it disappeared, only to be replaced by an engorged, vibrating cock bristling with splinters. More chunks of wood fell to the floor as several cocks, dripping with precum, punched gloryholes through the door.

"They want to fuck us to death, Daddy," Jasmine screamed as the bedroom door rocked on its weakened hinges. "How could they be so mean to me? I love animals." A note of defiance had crept into her voice and Demetri's head jerked around. She sounded like her mother, and she looked like Marian as she stood with one hand on her hip, the other flicking her long, blond hair from her pretty, pouting face.

"It must have been that shit Old Ed sold me from China. Instead of poison, it's some mad concoction of growth hormones and Viagra for bunny breeding farms. Fucking Old Ed, the stupid bastard… I'll go first to test the mattress." Demetri leapt onto the window ledge and peered at the concrete far below. He glanced back over his shoulder to reassure Jasmine there was a good chance this could work.

Behind her, several rabbit cocks hammered the gloryholes like pneumatic drills. Demetri jumped from the window, landed on the mattress, and rolled onto the concrete. He looked up at Jasmine. She was squatting on the window ledge, clutching at the curtains. "For fuck's sake jump, you silly bitch," he yelled and waved his arms, beckoning her to leap down.

"It looks scary. I might get hurt."

"You'll get hurt much worse if you stay there."

"Can't you lead them away or something, Daddy? Make them chase you so I can escape."

Demetri heard the bedroom door crash to the floor, and a herd of rabbits stampeded into the room. Jasmine screamed and jumped from the window ledge, flapping her arms in an attempt to fly. She overshot the mattress and her legs shattered as she hit the concrete, feet first. The tops of her tibias jutted through her knees on impact. "Oh god, help me, Daddy," Jasmine whined as she lay on the ground sprawled out in the shape of a swastika. "Don't let the bunnies fuck me."

Demetri looked toward the tractor and then back to his daughter. In fifty steps he could be a free man, free from the burden of his family, but it was his daughter lying there helpless that made him hesitate. His darling whose hand he'd held when she took her first step. He moved towards her. Blood seeped through her t-shirt emblazoned with the words 'Vegans save lives'. His eyes narrowed, then he spun around and ran to the tractor. "Daddy, nooo! Come back, you fucker!"

The tractor had been torn apart. Huge chunks had been ripped from the tires. The engine lay upended on a bed of tangled wires and leaked fuel. Marian's BMW and his pickup truck were parked in the barn. Demetri sprinted across the field as the giant rabbits appeared on the front porch. On reaching the barn, he turned and saw Jasmine barely visible beneath a mass of thrusting rabbits. They tore at her clothes and rammed their steely erections at her from all angles. Her screams of "I'm a vegan, I'm a vegan" were carried on the breeze.

A dozen rabbits hopped down from the barn roof. Demetri shouldered through the door and barred it. His pickup truck and Marian's car had been sabotaged. The rabbits thumped on the outside of the barn door. Demetri snatched the angle grinder laying on a workbench and flicked the switch. It whirred into life.

The wooden planks splintered and gnashing teeth appeared through the gaps. The barn walls rattled to their foundations.

Phalluses replaced teeth through the holes in the barn door. Demetri charged forward and brought the spinning grinder disc down onto a rabbit's cockhead. Prick meat splattered over Demetri's face and clothes. He swept the angle grinder across the length of the barn door, sanding and grinding a multitude of cocks and rabbit faces. Demetri was up to his ankles in gore by the time the last attacker had succumbed. He let out a sigh of relief and turned off the angle grinder.

The barn door was suddenly torn away from its hinges and thrown across the field. Standing among the debris of mangled rabbit flesh was a figure so enormous it blocked out the sun behind it. A rabbit at least sixteen feet tall crouched at the entrance to the barn. Demetri stared in wide-eyed horror. The monster lumbered toward him. Its teeth were the size of swords and its cock resembled a felled tree trunk. The piss hole oozed a trail of slimy precum. Cockless rabbits filed after the mega-giant mutant bunny as it closed in on Demetri. He had nowhere to go. He tried to switch the angle grinder back on, but it didn't respond. A groan rumbled from the monster's throat that shook the ground beneath Demetri's feet. He shrank away until his back pressed against his pickup truck.

He raised his fists and braced himself, but his legs were jelly and his body shook in terror. The beast swiped at him. Demetri was flung backwards and spreadeagled over the bonnet. Sharp claws shredded his jeans and sliced into his thighs. "Oh fuck,

fuck, no don't!" Demetri tightened his sphincter as a cockhead the size of a stormtrooper's helmet tried to invade his asshole. He couldn't believe what was happening. How could his mama and papa back in the old country show their faces in the village when everyone eventually found out their son, who'd gone to make a better life for himself and his family abroad, had been raped to death by a giant bunny rabbit?

Blinding agony engulfed Demetri as his colon was annihilated by the monster rabbit's swollen pole. His bowels released a torrent of faecal sludge onto the barn floor, splashing his boots with foamy, brown shit. Air wheezed out of his lungs as the mighty prick broke through the wall of his large intestine and ruptured his stomach. His guts burst and green, putrid-smelling bile flooded out of his mouth like toxic waste. An audience of voyeuristic, eunuch rabbits gathered around Demetri and rubbed the bloody stumps between their legs. With each thrust, Demetri's innards were pushed upwards until he puked out his lungs. He used the last of his strength to turn his head and gaze into the rabbit rapist's bulging, dead eyes. Tides of bunny batter blasted the final remnants of Demetri's insides from his mouth and across the exterior of his pickup truck.

CHOMPEr

One thing you may not be aware of about tooth fairies is that teeth are like cocaine to us. In the fairy kingdom, we call this good shit 'Chomper'. We go crazy for the stuff. You have to know your limits though, otherwise it can make you a little loopy. Trust me, I've seen many a fairy get hooked on the stuff then become inept, retarded, and even die. Being a tooth fairy requires a certain level of professionalism, you know. If you can't do the job properly, what use are you? Might as well be living under a bridge like a troll. So, the Queen now forbids us to snort it. Greedy bitch wants to keep it all for herself. She sits on her throne all day, strung out on the pearly white goodness, looking like Tony Montana. Not this time, though. This is my last day. After seven hundred and forty-seven years and the honour of being the Oberfairy of Auschwitz's tooth fairy camp, I'm retiring.

First stop is Jimmy Jessop's house. He lost his front tooth biting into a stale candy bar. Luckily for him, it was one of his milk teeth. We always leave a bit of extra green when the tooth has fallen out from misadventure. Jimmy will wake up with a crisp twenty under his pillow in the morning. Not that he needs it; the kid's doing pretty well it seems. He's got a nice house, right in the middle of suburbia. The kind of place I wouldn't mind spending my retirement in. The single dwelling is situated under the vast shadow of a leafy, giant oak tree. A white picket fence surrounds the property. It's nice, but I'd install some razor wire along the top of it to keep out the cats and the foreigners. Yep, I can definitely see myself living in digs like this. I wonder if he's got a butler? I'd have one.

He's left his bedroom window slightly ajar. Silly cunt. I don't condone such carelessness. You never know what weirdo will sneak in given half a chance. I adjust my balls in my lace panties, hitch up my pink tutu and tool belt, and try to squeeze through the gap. It's a tight fit. I admit I'm not as slender as I used to be, but I suck in my gut and after a few grunts, I'm inside. Jimmy snores in his bed. The sleep apnea machine whirrs softly beside him. Chocolate bar wrappers and scrunched up crisp packets litter his mattress. He looks like a bloated elephant stranded on top of a fucking landfill.

I love fucking with sleeping, fat kids. I buzz over to the machine and detach the nozzle that sends air to his mask. I pull up my tutu, stretch my panties aside to expose my puckered, bright orange asshole, and let rip. My fart ripples down the rubber tube. A fairy's flatulence is a notoriously noxious substance. We used to use it all the time in Auschwitz, but I bet you won't read about that in any history book. I smirk and re-attach the tube. Wide-eyed, I watch the specks of glittery fecal matter dance around in the transparent mask before disappearing up Jimmy's flared nostrils. He gags and splutters violently into his breathing apparatus.

Enough messing around, I want to snort his tooth up bad. The enamel nugget is under his pillow, sealed in a zip lock bag. Ugh. My little fingers can never open these things. I grab my Stanley knife and slit open the plastic. Jimmy's been a lazy little prick and not been cleaning his teeth properly. The tooth is piss-yellow and has a big ass cavity. Still, I pop the twenty under the pillow and retreat to a desk in the corner. I whip out my hammer to pulverise my prize. Jimmy stirs from all the noise as I crush the tooth to a fine dust but doesn't awaken. The Chomper is an ugly colour from all the rot. I'd have much preferred some pure white, but I'm keen to sample the goods anyway. I thumb one nostril and vacuum up a long line.

Chomper roars through my sinuses and I snap my head back like a whip. Oooh, it's good. Really fucking good. My insides blaze. The veins in my temple pulse and my eyes bulge. Pressed against the soft fabric of my panties, my tumescent cock fights for release. It suddenly juts out of the tutu, salivating a gloopy pre-cum from a dilated pisshole. My willy may only be the length of a human thumbnail but in the fairy world, that's a very impressive size. I even wrecked Tinkerbell's asshole with it back when we were dating. She has to fly around clutching a colostomy bag now, and she still refuses to talk to me. "I'm a fucking chomped up fairy fuck machine," I yell. But first I want some more Chomper.

Wielding the hammer tightly, I dart from the desk towards Jimmy's chubby face. I tear his mask off. Jimmy's eyes spring open and he lets out a girly shriek when he sees me hovering above him like the angel of death. Before he can comprehend this waking nightmare, I drive the hammer down onto his mouth, smashing teeth, lips, and jawbone. Blow after savage blow, the lower part of his pudgy face crumples inwards like a sinkhole. Blood spews from his mangled jaw.

He tries to grab at the flaps of blubber that were his cheeks. Shards of teeth poke through his skin and glorious streaks of crimson graffiti the bedroom walls. "Gimme those teeth, you fat cunt," I scream at him. His eyes are pools of anguished tears, but I don't give a fuck. I want Chomper. I lust for it more than anything right now. My steel toe cap boot finds his quivering, soft chin, and I dislodge several teeth at the same time from his bloody gums.

"Mummy, Mummy." Jimmy gurgles the words out of his pummelled mouth like a cum slut after a gangbang. Fat hands swat at me but I'm much too fast. He flops out of bed. The floor shudders under his weight. He drags himself across the floor on his belly, trying to push through the discarded rubbish. That'll teach you, Jimmy. You should have cleaned your room. The terrified boy hoists himself up and edges towards the door on his hands and knees. "Mummy, Mummy, the tooth fairy came," he whimpers deliriously.

I saw at his Achilles tendons with my Stanley knife. The flesh is as soft as warm butter. He thuds to the ground, a writhing maggot urinating into his pyjama bottoms. He rolls over and I clamber up the wheezing walrus. I stand defiantly on his undulating belly, all his teeth now in my possession. I drag the blade from his bitch tits down to his navel. A gaping chasm of fatty tissue opens up, and his glistening, wet organs gleam in the moonlight shining through the window. The wheezing stops and he lies still. I consider taking the twenty back, but decide to leave it under the pillow. I've got the teeth. I'll have enough Chomper for weeks.

My cock throbs angrily, still unsatisfied. Chomper makes fairies so fucking horny. I drop the milk teeth into my fairy yarn sack and squeeze my pulsating meat. "Don't worry, big boy, I'm going to get you some pussy. Just hang tight. Mummy must be around here somewhere." I fucking love milf cunt. Fairy pussy is nice and sweet but you can't beat a lovely piece of human hole, especially one that's birthed a big, fat twat like Jimmy Jessop. Damn, Jimmy's door is closed. I fumble around with the knob for a minute before the latch clicks.

A long corridor stretches before me. A net curtain blows ethereally in a night breeze. The passageway opens to a bedroom on the left with a sky-blue ceiling and ivory walls. Much to my disappointment, the crib inside is empty.

Two shapes sleep in the next bedroom. I recall their names from my itinerary as I hover above them. The woman is Leeanne. The man snoring beside her is Brian. Leeanne is a looker. She's all long, black hair, and her freckled face is embellished with a cute, pierced, chipmunk nose that I want to stick right up my ass. First though, I must deal with Brian. I can't have some cunt like him spoiling my fun with his wife. If I'm to enjoy my last night on the job as a tooth fairy, I'm going to have to ensure she can't run away either. Two matching floral dressing gowns hang on hooks beside the wardrobe. Geez, I thought my tutu looked gay but it's nothing compared to Brian's dressing gown. Their woven belts will make ideal ropes. I fasten the cords around Leeanne's ankles and wrists carefully so as not to wake her. It doesn't take me long to tie her to the bed.

I zoom under the covers and into the open fly of Brian's boxer shorts. His limp, shrivelled dick is nuzzled up against his bush of wiry, ginger pubes. I need that cock pumped full of blood for what I intend to do with it, so I give it a little rub and tickle.

"Ooh, mmm," Brian groans. I grasp his swelling phallus with both hands and shake it vigorously. "Ooh, yeah, nasty girl, squeeze my balls too. You know how I like that shit. Mmm, squeeze harder. Harder, I said. Yes, that's it. Right there. Ooh, ooh, fuck. Tongue my crown." I don't mind giving Brian a handjob, but there's no way I'm going to lick his cockhead. No amount of Chomper will change that.

His prick quickly unfurls. As it stands to attention, I slash at the root with my knife. Brian jerks awake and sits bolt upright in the bed. His severed manhood collapses onto his belly. Black blood spurts out of the wound at a regular rhythm and soaks his shorts and wife. He lets out a banshee wail as he fumbles around for his detached member. Pathetic cunt. I take the opportunity to neuter him as Leeanne is startled awake and realises she's not able to go anywhere. Her screams coalesce with her husband's own feminine cries.

Brian flicks the switch on a bedside lamp. He stares, ashen, at the blotchy, curled piece of useless meat cupped in his trembling hands. I throw the testicles at him and they bounce off his face and roll under the bed. Brian sees me and screams again. He's so pallid, I think he's going to faint. Leeanne thrashes against her bonds. Her luscious, milk-white titties jiggle like two plates of blancmange left out in a gale.

I shoot straight at Brian, my Stanley knife at the ready. The blade sinks into his windpipe, stifling his scream. A geyser of blood squirts out of the hole like a cumshot over his wife's sobbing face. Gravity yanks him straight down to the blood-stained carpet. He spasms like a menstruating epileptic, his dead dick firmly in his grasp.

The Chomper is still coursing relentlessly through my eight-inch body. The milf's wide, wet, sexy green eyes stare at me as I dive-bomb into her wobbly orbs. Her whole body shakes violently. The tremors make my magical meatstick seep an endless river of bubbling pre-cum. I tear her nightie open. Her tits are jelly mountains. I scale one, and as I reach the summit, I jump up and down on the the pink, pimply rubber teat as if it's a trampoline. She glares at me, mumbling some shit about rape, as I spit in my hand and watch myself work long strokes along my veiny shaft in the reflection of her dilated pupils. She's mesmerised by me and jabbers wildly. I splatter her eyelids with frothy fluid. As much fun as I'm having, it's pussy I want.

I depart from her breast and float down to her shaved, meaty snatch. She's lying in a damp patch where she's pissed herself in fright. Fuck, I love the heady aroma of human cunt flaps drenched in salty piss.

You may very well be wondering how sex between a fairy and a human works. I'll explain in a moment, but first I need to get myself well-oiled in this milf's vaginal drippings. My hands part her labia majora like a pair of red velvet drapes. Her fuckhole gapes, and I burrow into the blackness of her sex. I'm shaped like a good-sized dildo, so I squeeze into the cavity. My fairy wings tickle her walls and her insides moisten. I can hear the squelch beneath my boots as I tread blindly along her vaginal canal, stoned off my tits on Chomper, and drawn ever onwards by the stench of her cervix. I lap at the soggy pussy flesh all around me, tasting the parts of this bitch's fuckhole that she's unable to clean properly without the aid of a vaginal douche. My outstretched fingers find the cervix. I reach into my tool belt and locate a torch. I press the on button and a blinding beam illuminates Leeanne's insides. The inner depths of her cunt resemble a slimy cave. Stalactites of translucent syrup dangle above me. Her cervix looks like a large, glazed donut. I peek into the dimple, using the torchlight to scan the contents of her womb.

"Well, well, well, what do we have here?" Leeanne is pregnant. A foetus the same size as me floats in an embryonic sac. The ugly motherfucker is giving me the side eye. "What you staring at me like that for?"

Out comes the Stanley knife. I carve open the sac and hold on to a fallopian tube as the fluid gushes out so I don't get swept away by the tsunami. The baby flaps around like a fish out of water in Leeanne's cavernous womb. The tip of my boot connects with the head, and I bash it in until the nascent face turns into a thick, lumpy paste. The joy of tenderising this unborn kid makes my heart thump hard in my chest. This is a hatchet job for sure. I swap the knife for the tool I typically use for stubborn window panes and hack the limbs off. Now the stupid fucker looks like a thalidomide baby. I haven't seen anything so repulsive-looking since I had the job of collecting teeth from the orphanage in Chernobyl. Now, I'm not the sentimental type, but I don't want the cunt to live its short, debilitating life as a helpless retard, so I karate chop its fragile skull with the hatchet.

I squeeze my way out of Leeanne's cunt. I'm sticky from head to toe. Pussy slime fills my nostrils and ears. It's all I can taste and smell. This is fucking heaven. Her pee hole spews out more droplets of golden piss. This big-titted cumrag is frozen in fear. This makes me ravenous with desire. The thought of her miscarriage almost makes me blow my load early. I slap my cock then thrust it into her urethra. "Fuck me, your pee hole feels like it's lined with silk. And it's so tight! It's better than Tink's virgin asshole. Uhhhhh!"

Flapping my wings, I spin upside down so I can confront Leeanne's asshole. I punch my fist into her browneye until it loosens enough that I can bury my face in it. My cock pounds her pisser while I eat my fill of bitter shit. Delicious. Did you know Chomper stimulates your tastebuds like a motherfucker? The woman howls in agony. I'm the worst urinary tract infection she's ever had. She queefs in fright and the slurry of her dead baby oozes out between her thighs. I'm buzzing from the stench and the mess. Thank you, Jimmy. Thank you for having a mouth full of foul, rotten teeth. This is the best Chomper I've ever snorted.

I can't let this bitch live after all she's witnessed. She might report me to the fairy authorities. They can't fire me, but they might dock my severance or slap me with a heavy fine. I can't let that happen. I want to live comfortably in my retirement. I want to get into property and find myself a nice, little place like this with a white picket fence and a giant oak tree. I want a butler.

Leeanne is sopping wet so she clearly likes a rough fucking. I don't think she was getting it from ginger Brian. My tiny hand wraps around the bedside lamp. I pull off the shade, smash the bulb against the bedside table and ram the lamp deep into her bloody cunt. She screams so loudly the windows rattle. I force the lamp into this bitch's fuckhole until the round, metal base squashes her labia and her pussy emits a lengthy fart. The black electrical cord trails away from her cunt like it's the string of a tampon. She begs me to stop, shaking her head from side to side as the jagged bulb carves up her pussy walls. Her eyes roll back in her head. "Oh my god, stop, you're killing me!" she groans.

I jackhammer her gaping hole with the lamp. My finger finds the switch and I flip it. Leeanne spazzes around on the mattress as the volts shoot through her body. Her cunt crackles and hisses as I fuck her with her bedside light. Black smoke billows out of her ravaged gash and the smog hits me in the face. I cough from the fumes. Her ass slides over the remains of her mashed up baby and the pulpy mess sticks to her butt cheeks. Blood bubbles out of her orifice. Flames lick from it and she begins to smell like barbecued meat.

"Mmm, such a delicious aroma. I like my pussy cooked well done." Green-brown vomit flows from the sides of her mouth. The skin blisters and blackens. Orange flames blaze through the charred, cracked flesh and her tits burst open. The titty fat crackles and I lick my lips hungrily. I'm starving. Chomper gives you a severe case of the munchies, don't you know? A cloud of smoke pours from between her lips. I chuckle as I'm once again reminded of my days as Oberfairy at Auschwitz. The smoke rose from the chimneys all day long. Good times.

I leave the bitch still smoking and the lamp halfway up her cunt. I fly back to Jimmy's bedroom, grab the sack of teeth, and head for the open window, excited by the prospect of retirement and having acquired a copious amount of Chomper to snort at my leisure. A black shape bolts out from the shadows. "Oh shit," I shriek. "A fucking cat!" Cats are the mortal enemies of tooth fairies. Many a fairy has been lost in the line of duty, fatalities due to felines.

I drop the sack and make haste for the exit. The cat pounces. I take evasive manoeuvres but I'm not quick enough. The claws scrape my wings, leaving them in tatters. Shit, I'm fucked. As I fly around in a big circle, descending to the ground, the cat wiggles on its haunches.

The fucker springs and a paw swats me from the air. I spiral to the ground, dizzy and unable to avoid a crash landing. I narrowly miss Jimmy's corpse and hit the floor hard. An agonising pain corkscrews through my right arm as it snaps at the elbow. My left leg bends the wrong way and winds up behind my head. I hear the cat's purr get increasingly louder as I lie next to an empty packet of cheese and onion crisps, trying desperately to retrieve my trusty Stanley knife. I grit my teeth and grab it.

The cat bats the blade from my hand with a look of indifference on its goddamn face. I seize the hammer and try to keep the feline at bay, but it's no good. The cat's ears flatten and the weapon is whacked away from my grasp again. This kitty knows how to fight.

Jaws close around me. Pointed teeth puncture my chest and hot pain stabs through my upper body. Huge, yellow eyes stare at me as I writhe in the vice-like hold of the cat's unwavering mouth. I can't breathe. My little lungs have been impaled by the family pet. Frothy blood bubbles out of me. I try to suck in and blow out air, but all I can feel is the cat clamping down with more force. Its back arches and the tail lashes at the air. Unsheathed claws rake my flesh as I drag myself to a low space under a nearby dresser.

I'm batted around a few more times as everything darkens around me. The cat's mouth cracks open in a full-throated yawn. I can't defend myself. I'm a fucking crippled fairy. The cat looks bored with its plaything. Maybe it'll fuck off and bother a mouse or something. Breathing is even more difficult now, almost impossible. I don't have the strength to make it to the open window. I'm not sure I'll make it home. If I could only get another hit of Chomper to ease the searing pain…

The cat's paw weighs down on my chest. I'm pinned where I lie. I stare up at the ridged roof of its open mouth, moving closer.

Those dagger teeth close over my head. The mouth is my death shroud. Leeanne's pussy smell has diminished too. All I can sense now is the hot stench of a cat's stinking breath as darkness envelops me, and another fairy dies.

Simon McHardy is the author of the infamous MOTHER MAGGOT. He lives a reclusive life in Tasmania Australia.

Find him at Amazon and godless

Sean Hawker writes depraved splatterpunk novellas, novelettes, and short stories. He's won a couple awards for his literary filth. He lives in Gloucestershire, England with two albinos and a midget.

Find him at Amazon and godless

Printed in Great Britain
by Amazon

22906167R00101